T0194312

anxious pleasures

Also by Lance Olsen

anxious pleasures

a novel after kafka

Lance Olsen

COUNTERPOINT

BERKELEY

Library of Congress Cataloging-in-Publication Data

Olsen, Lance, 1956–
Anxious pleasures : a novel after Kafka / Lance Olsen.
p. cm.
Kafka's Metamorphosis reanimated through the vantage points
of those who surrounded Gregor Samsa during his plight.
ISBN-13: 978-1-59376-135-6
ISBN-10: 1-59376-135-X
I. Kafka, Franz, 1883–1924. Metamorphosis. II. Title.
PS3565.L777A85 2007
813'.54—dc22

2006030688

Book design by Gopa & Ted2, Inc.
Printed in the United States of America

COUNTERPOINT
2560 Ninth Street Suite 318
Berkeley, CA 94710
counterpointpress.com

for Andi,

memory's collaborator

Remembering is a form of forgetting.

—Milan Kundera, *Testaments Betrayed*

grete

—quarter to seven, Gregor, says Mutti from the hallway. Weren't you supposed to catch your train, dear?

Hanging in the soft grayness between sleep and waking, I listen for a little while to her voice, the heavy raindrops slapping the windowpane, the tram clanking several blocks away.

Then a vivid stillness presses in, as if someone were waiting on the other side of my big brother's door, deliberately refusing to answer, and I know something isn't right.

They say the time you spend in a foreign country isn't part of your own life. The same is true with music and dreaming. You live somewhere else as someone else and never want to leave. The shock is how, when you finally do, you discover everything in exactly the same place as before. What an extraordinary act of will: to seize hold of the contents of the room around you just where you left them, as though you have never been gone, the instant of coming back the riskiest of the day.

—*Gregor,* Papa's voice joins in from the living room. He is unintentionally loud like the deaf. You want to tell him, *Calm down, Papa, we can all hear you very well,* but he can't help it. His voice is naturally clumsy, the way a reindeer looks.

—What's the matter with you? he is asking. What's going on in there?

He is knocking quietly on my big brother's door, yet using his fist.

I listen, not wanting to rouse, step up onto the shore of a

fresh day, but next, in the gap between two breaths, I find my-self standing beside my bed, pulling my dark dress with the pretty embroidered chrysanthemums on the collar over my head, searching for my shoes. It is still dark outside. The only light is the pale sheen on the ceiling and upper surfaces of furniture cast by electric lamps from the street below. The rainy morning makes our flat seem as if it has somehow fallen out of alignment.

When he was my age, Gregor's favorite subject at the Gym-nasium was geography. Isn't that funny? He used to read Sven Hedin's accounts of his voyages to the far corners of the earth. The cannibals in the South Pacific who during feasts spat out their enemies' teeth onto the sand around them like cherry pits. The stringy parasites in Asia that twist across the whites of your eyes on their swim toward your thoughts.

After he returned from the service, he lost interest in such things. He never left this province again. And all that chat-ter about travel. All that business about seeing the world. He started talking about taking a degree in chemistry instead. Chemistry! And Gregor having done so frightfully in math.

Still, when Papa got into trouble, Gregor changed his mind straightaway and became a traveling salesman in cloth. There was no discussion, no weighing of options. It happened so rap-idly you would have thought it was what he had been planning all along. He became a traveling salesman and, soon as he could afford it, found us this flat divided into regular segments like—like a brown bug's belly, Georg would have said. If he were still with us. If this flat had somehow been aligned differently.

I was twelve. Then I was seventeen. Like dreaming or music, when you are gliding through those years, they feel they will never end. Once they are finished with you, you have such a difficult time recalling them in any sort of detail it seems they very well may have happened to a friend you no longer see, and you just heard about them secondhand, or maybe you read about them in a letter. It isn't you anymore. Imagine all the people you no longer are.

Gregor looked down at his hands with those long, thin, pretty fingers of his when I asked him why he did it, why he became a traveling salesman overnight, and he said:

—That's what brothers are supposed to do, isn't it?

He didn't seem sure of the answer himself.

Gregor works very hard. He has never reported in sick a day in his life. Every morning at 4 AM, hanging far back in that soft grayness, I hear his alarm rattle alive next door. If I concentrate, I can just sense myself rolling over, tugging up the covers to my chin, snuggling back into the drowsy warmth, and then I am away again.

Until this morning, that is.

Until now.

Because something isn't right. Mutti is speaking at the door leading into Gregor's room from the hallway. Her voice is kind yet uneasy. An asthmatic rasp has colored it a phlegmy amber. I can hear her shuffling back and forth in place in her delft-blue robe, doing a nervous waltz with herself.

She is a piccolo, Papa an oboe. They are playing the same tune, but in different keys. My big brother is a rest held bar after bar. There is no reply from his room, only a silence not so much silence as a sound waiting to express itself.

My stomach crumples into a jackdaw trapped inside a wooden box. Passing my window, buttoning my dress, I glance down at the hospital across Charlotte Street. The pavement beneath the electric lamps is so wet it looks as polished as

Gregor's desktop. Stone-gray in the rain, the long low building stretches on down the block until it disappears altogether in the dim fog like an imperfect memory.

My brain spiderwebby, I cross to the door connecting my room with Gregor's. I lean my forehead against the cool white paint, listening to my parents' voices, inhaling last evening's cabbage and the too-warm sour fumes from the coal-burning tile stove.

Eyes shut, picking at the frayed cuticle on my right index finger, I wait for a lull and ask gently into the darkness:

—Gregor? Aren't you well? It's Grete, Gregor. Is there anything I can get you?

Two breaths, two breaths more, and my big brother replies.

mutti

What in the world did he — couldn't understand a word — if
he doesn't get up soon he's going to miss his train — and then
where will we all be — but the doctor — he told me have
yourself a bit of a lie-down — think of somewhere nice he
said — easy for *him* I shouldn't wonder — standing there in
that fancy coat of his — can't think of a single thing — except
how my lungs are hardening — when did this old bag of bones
— when did it begin pulling such applesauce — but he used
to watch out for us didn't he — hair so blond it was white
— vanilla scent when he sweats — my shortbread boy — and
now — locking his door from the inside — refusing to answer
his own father — when did it come down to this — the way
he used to huddle beneath the dining table for hours — playing dominos by himself — sherry-brown eyes looking right
into your secrets — children used to put on those one-acts for
my birthday — miniature kings and queens and paper castles
— we had such times together — Sunday afternoons in the
park — white light blinking through the branches — Gregor
and Georg and Grete holding hands — Papa's face flushed with
sunshine — we followed them down the gravel path — our
hearts big red balloons of pride — *this is what we have done*
— we wanted to tell everyone — *this is what we've accomplished*
— what mother could wish for more — a handful of moments
like those in her life — no use gritching is it — that plus a
handful of pfennigs — they'll get you a nice pig's knuckle from

the butcher boy — *Gregor,* Papa is saying from the living room — *enough of this nonsense* — *open the door this instant* — and how in the beginning I used to ask him — me only seventeen — I used to ask him — tell me what it was like over there — and he'd just look at me across the table — as though I hadn't said a thing — wouldn't frown mind you — wouldn't make me feel queer for the asking — just looked at me — as though he didn't know I'd been sitting there all along — and then start talking about something else entirely — *did you have a chance to speak to Mrs. Marsten today,* he'd say — *about extending our credit* — the worlds he has seen — I shouldn't wonder — girl needs a man like that — *China* for goodness sakes — *rickshaws* — and me all marmalade and six kinds of bad lungs inside — give it half an hour — no more — and Gregor will be on his way to work — I'm sure of it — the rest of us sitting around the breakfast table — I'll ask the cook to fry us up some eggs — eggs and toast — sausages as well — because after the rains set in — autumn doesn't do much for people with an appetite for color does it — that's why the Lord created spring — gives you something to look forward to — the extra sleep will do him good — fighting off a bit of a cold — happens to us all — barely hangs up his bowler in the foyer — before he's kissing Grete and me goodbye again — because — and what's *that* now — what's *that* he's doing — ?

ραπα

He's trying to make fools of us all, The Father thinks, fist falling a final time against the white swing door. I simply won't have it. Not in my house.

For the past five years The Father has loved nothing more than rising gradually into each morning, letting the bright presence of the day incrementally tint his consciousness. The shrill scent of coffee and oranges. Two greasy links of sausage. He has loved nothing more than taking his own good time over his toilet, lathering in the mirror above the washbasin, shaving with precision, and, at length, strolling out to the living room to linger with his wife and daughter over a delicious breakfast.

The morning glides by, punt down a river, and, before you know it, you are occupying afternoon light. What is the passage of minutes for, half a decade into retirement, if not to relish the world like this? Youth burns itself up believing there's no end to time, but blind boys shouldn't judge colors.

At this age, here, The Father has come to understand that the ticking of his pocket watch is all about enjoying his pocket watch's ticking. He has done his bit. No one can quarrel with him on that score. The Father has jolly well earned the right to dally over the newspaper, catch up on the latest about the war, see what developments occurred while his swath of the planet lay shawled.

It is easy to be brave from a safe distance, but The Father was there. He has seen things. How at night, as he lay in his cot in the stinking muddy trench in Burma, he could sometimes hear the *pop . . . pop . . . pop* coming across the no-man's land from the village captured earlier that day, as the bastards lined up the children against bamboo walls and shot them in the feet so they couldn't grow up to be soldiers.

The puppy yaps as the bullets broke bone.

The Father has done his bit, and more. And what, precisely, do he and his country have to show for it? It is not by any means simple to say. Back when theories seemed to matter, some maintained the enemy had committed itself to destroying our language and thereby our thought, others that it wanted nothing more than to enter our dreams because, until then, we had never dreamed about them, although they had dreamed about us almost every night.

The Father saw things, although what specifically those things were he cannot be at all certain. Read enough newspapers, listen to enough politicians, and soon what you thought you had observed smudges into newsprint and the static of patriotic speeches on the radio. Tell a lie long enough, and it becomes the truth—or, if not quite that, then at least a half-truth in which people find it increasingly easy to believe.

In the early days, the regime referred to the bastards as *the barbarians*. Later, under pressure from the left, it began calling them, simply and impartially, *the natural disasters*. They were whirlwinds and earthquakes, only flesh. Few citizens had actually seen them, and most of those, like the children in that village, seldom used words again. If they did, the stories they recited conflicted with the stories recited by others in similar circumstances. It was as if each victim had witnessed something altogether unique. So the only fact that remained consistent was this: the regime was under attack by those who wanted to make its lives into their lives, or perhaps into no lives at all, and every morning, lingering over breakfast, The Father thumbed through the newspapers, looking for something that passed for illumination because he deserved nothing less. He was continually disappointed.

He happens for a brief moment to catch sight of the three photographs framed on the wall behind the dining table. Fresh out of training, hand on sword, a lanky Gregor wears the remains of a smile in the first. Two days after the photograph was taken, he shipped out for the front just as The Father had done three decades before. Eighteen months later, the doorbell rang. The young man on the landing looked like The Father's son. He sounded like The Father's son. Yet The Father was convinced the army had sent back a stranger in his boy's place. Gregor immediately started squandering his days at the café, talking all that bollocks about attending university. It took the full weight of The Father's misfortune (nearly thirty years at a decent trade gone with a single sentence uttered almost in passing by his snub-nosed superior) to wake Gregor from his fantasies and place him back in honest work.

If The Father had had it to do over again, he would have sent him away to the military academy despite his wife's protestations. It would have made all the difference. A childhood there, and Gregor would have learned ability is the poor man's wealth. But at this age, half a decade into retirement, the only thing to do is try to believe this isn't a particularly bad place to have ended up, standing here in this living room, hands in the pockets of his robe, coaxing his own flesh and blood to unlock the door and let him in.

The photograph of Georg, hanging below and left of Gregor's, was taken shortly after he got involved in all that starving business. The skin on his cheeks already tugs tighter against its skeletal architecture than is strictly healthy. His dark brown eyes have already begun to sink back into his head on their expedition to another place. As a child, he used to fritter away his time on the sofa, studying those silly books, but when push came to shove he found himself a proper means of employment—if you can call sitting in a cage full of hay in the town square for weeks on end while people gawk and point and laugh at you a proper means of employment.

The thought flickers across The Father's awareness that he is, truth to tell, glad Georg is not here to see this embarrassment. Or add to it. There is already enough worry to fill this flat, and, right around the next corner, down the next hallway, there will be more.

The Father's useless daughter, for instance. Only *now* is she thinking of pitching in. Who raised these children? Surely not The Father. He was busy earning a decent day's wage. Just look at her, roosting in the chair in that photograph with her daft violin, looking serious and poised in the manner only sixteen-year-old girls without a clue about existence can look serious and poised.

The time. The money. The very idea makes The Father blink so fiercely the tips of his chalky mustache rise. In hard times, a man needs someone he can depend on. The Father learned this in the trenches, the way men did, listening to that *pop . . . pop . . . pop* arriving in the night. Yet all he has surrounding him is a flat full of dullards trying to make a fool of him.

Maybe you have to love them because they are yours, but you certainly don't have to fancy them much.

The Father becomes aware of the front doorbell ringing. He understands at once it spells further trouble. If it's not one thing, it's one hundred. No one comes around at this hour unless it's a delivery or an emergency. The insistence of this ringing means it is no delivery.

The Father summons the servant girl and instructs her to answer. She stalls at the living room entrance, staring at him with that bland, blank, pitted, pinkish face, as if staring at a dozen eggs that have just rolled off the countertop and splattered on the floor, and then evaporates without indicating whether or not she has understood a thing he's said.

The Father listens to her footfalls moving down the hallway and feels momentarily invisible.

He scowls.

His ping-pong-paddle hands re-fist.

the servant girl

The chief clerk stands on the landing, wringing out his umbrella. He is even taller than Mr. Samsa and looks like a cross between an undertaker and a basset hound. He doesn't meet my eyes. He doesn't say a word. He just surveys the hall behind me over my head, waiting for me to step out of his way.

I don't know who he is, but I know who he is. I curtsy fast and shallow in case he happens to drop his attention to my height. He doesn't. I ask him if he would like to see the master of the house.

He just stands there, wringing, waiting.

Last night I dreamed I was on the bank of the river. All the lights in the city were out. A little boy in a sailor suit stood beside me. He pointed to the water and said:

—See the rowboat out there? Your mother is in it. She is dying. Save her.

It was less a rowboat than a white glimmer hanging in the night. Maybe I could swim to it, even though I didn't know how to swim. Maybe I could figure what to do as I went along. I stepped off the bank into the water and sank straight down. Tangled in the seaweed on the bottom, I waved my arms around my head like I was swatting away bees, only very slowly.

This will only last a few seconds, I told myself. *Then it will be done.*

I tried to relax, but a large strong hand grabbed me by the

hair and yanked me up. It was my mother. We were in the rowboat. She wasn't wearing any clothes. Her thingies were fish-floppy and almost touched her bellybutton.

—Happy birthday, angel, she said. In the fight between you and the world, back the world.

The dreams the natural disasters put into your mind.

I would forget them if I could, only they are the kind of dreams that won't let you go just because it happens to be dawn. All morning they hang on your back, misshapen children. The more you fight, the harder they grip.

Passing by me, the chief clerk reaches out and hangs his umbrella on my wrist as though I am a hat rack. His patent leather boots creak. They leave wet figure eights behind him.

I place the umbrella in the umbrella stand, lower myself onto my knees, and start wiping up the trail of numbers with my apron.

I can hear everyone talking in the living room. The chief clerk is saying when Gregor didn't appear for work on time, he hurried over. He asks Mr. Samsa did he understand it was already a quarter past seven, that the day, rain or no rain, was already in full swing.

In the middle of Mr. Samsa's reply, a heavy thump arrives from Gregor's room, like someone upended a heavy chair.

Everything in the flat becomes very still.

I stop wiping and raise my head.

—That was someone falling down, the chief clerk says.

—Gregor, says Mr. Samsa, the chief clerk is here, and he wants to know why you didn't catch the early train. We don't know what to tell him. He wants to talk to you in person. Open the door. He will be good enough to excuse the untidiness.

—Good morning, Mr. Samba, the chief clerk calls through the door.

The missus says something I can't hear, and the chief clerk replies:

—Quite right. I can't think of any other explanation, madam. He pauses. His voice changes. The false friendlessness slides out of it. Although, on the other hand, he continues, I must say that we men of business, fortunately or unfortunately, very often simply have to ignore this or that slight indisposition. One's duties must be attended to.

The missus says something else.

The master says, beginning to knock on the door again:

—Well, can the chief clerk come in now? Gregor?

In response, a second noise arrives. It reminds me of the one you make when you cut yourself unexpectedly. A surprised chirp.

—I must say, the chief clerk says, this really is no way to act. Here you are, barricading yourself in your room, causing your parents no end of worry. And—I mention this only in passing, of course—neglecting your responsibilities in a rather remarkable fashion. I was under the impression you were a quiet, dependable sort of person, the kind a company can rely on. But now all at once you seem bent on making a disgraceful exhibition of yourself. Perhaps I should take this opportunity to remind you that your position in the firm is not entirely invulnerable. Let me hasten to say I came with the intention of telling you all this in private, but since you are set on wasting everyone's time, I don't really see why your parents shouldn't hear it, too.

The missus says something else, her voice trembly. I finish wiping the floor, rise, and dry my hands on my apron.

—For quite some time, the chief clerk goes on, your work has been most unsatisfactory. Granted, this is not the season for a fiscal boom. I should be the first to admit it. Yet a season for doing no business at all? Such a season does not exist, Mr. Samba. Do I make myself perfectly clear?

Another thump from behind Gregor's door, a string of chirps.

—Oh, dear! cries the missus. My son's ill and we're merely tormenting him! Grete! Grete!

—Yes, Mutti?

—You must go for a doctor this minute! My darling isn't well!

They are calling to each other from different sides of Gregor's room. Mr. Samsa wolfs my name again. I count to ten and step forward. He is standing beside the chief clerk. They are both studying the closed door as if it is a huge, strange flower. Without turning around, Mr. Samsa instructs me to fetch a locksmith.

—Tell him it is urgent, he says over his shoulder.

—Yes, sir.

—But do not tell him what has happened. Simply tell him his presence is required immediately. Do you understand, Anna?

—Yes, sir.

—Off with you, then. Quickly now.

I get as far as the landing, my coat on, my hood up, before I remember the frightful weather outside. If I'm lucky, I'll cover half a block before being soaked through.

Grete flies past me, hollering as she goes:

—Hurry, Anna! Hurry! Gregor's in trouble!

—Yes, miss, I say, unmoving.

I don't know Gregor will open his door, but I know Gregor will open his door. Maybe he just stayed out too late with his friends. Maybe that's it. Maybe he forgot to set his alarm clock. No matter how ill you are, you can always walk three steps to unlock your door.

Standing there, listening to the rain falling outside, it occurs to me the locksmith can probably wait a little while longer. At least until the day clears a bit. But I should tell the cook what is going on. Otherwise she'll think I've run off and will be cross with me.

I count to ten again, contemplating the purchase of a new pair of shoes. I have my eyes set on the perfect ones. Black with bright brass buckles.

Maybe next month.

Next month or the month after.

I leave the door to the flat open behind me so they think I've dashed down the staircase, then double back into the flat, beelining for the kitchen before anyone sees.

the chief clerk

If commerce is a form of prayer, then any businessman worth his salt has a certain obligation to press forward toward fiscal enlightenment in the interest of his firm, regardless of a setback or two, no matter how ostensibly egregious, regardless of the way, say, he awoke alone in bed twelve days ago to discover the flat empty, his chubby wife gone with his little girl Lotte, a babyblue letter awaiting him on the armoire alleging that their life together had not been what their life together et cetera, or of the way, say, that his ten-hour workdays, six-day-a-week schedule (plus Sundays, when required), pledge to no private property in or upon his office desk, a fortnight's vacation every second year at the convenience of the company—the way that babyblue letter remained mute about these matters, choosing instead to accuse him of et cetera, while here he stands in this shabby room, all marshy barn-warmth, pressing forward beside a disheveled oaf still slothing about in his morning robe well past seven in the AM, although, were I to pass his recalcitrant son at the office, I confess I am not altogether confident I should be able to point him out to a co-worker, except perhaps to say that there is, I believe, something about him to do with a long tapering inverted triangle of a face, sharp cheeks, big ears, buggy brown eyes, if I am remembering the correct employee, and not someone else, something to do with how his desk is somewhat too small for him, giving passersby the impression of a gangling, stoop-shouldered young man riding a boy's bicycle, or with, I seem to recall, his most recent review, which concluded with the statement that his effort over the course of the year had been, at best, quote *minimally acceptable* unquote, although the truth seems to be I became aware of this, and him, only this past month, after the fellow apparently complained to an associate, who subsequently relayed the complaint to his superior, who subsequently relayed the complaint to me, that someone had conceivably tampered with the items on his, Samba's, de—

Ah, here we go: the lock.

The knob turning.

The door commencing to swing open.

grete

I rush the rest of the way down the stairs and out onto the pavement before fully grasping Anna isn't following me.

She was there, then she wasn't.

Retreating beneath the narrow overhang in front of the building, clinching my coat collar against the damp chill, I flutter back and forth between wanting to fetch the doctor and wanting to make sure the girl isn't dallying.

The rain has escalated from spatter to downpour, miniature white torrents luging along gutters.

Breathless, heart in flames, I picture my brother lying sick in bed and remember that night when he was seventeen and I seven and filled with flu and he crawled into my bed beside me and whispered into my fever dreams:

—Imagine an Emperor. He is the most powerful man in the land. He is dying on a great divan in a great chamber in his castle the size of our country. Even though you are just a poor handmaid living somewhere in the city beyond the gates, even though the Emperor has never met you, doesn't know your name, he feels he has an important message for you. With his last mouthful of life, he summons a herald and murmurs it into his ear just like I am doing into yours. The herald repeats the message but realizes he is already talking to a dead man. He kisses the Emperor's veined hand, crosses himself, and sets off. The hall outside the chamber is crammed with hundreds of people awaiting news. It takes the herald hours to make his way through. On the far side, he becomes lost among courtyards and alleys that go on and on in every direction. We skip. He grows old. He becomes conscious that beyond these courtyards and alleys there are more courtyards, and, beyond those, more. It will take him hundreds of years to navigate them, and then only if he happens to be traveling in the correct direction, although he isn't at all sure which direction that might be. And, if the herald succeeds, do you know what, Grete?

I shook my stuffy head no.

—He would still have to fight his way through further courtyards and alleys, into the outer palace, and, beyond that, the outer gate, and, beyond the outer gate, the snarled core of the capital city. And do you know how long this would take him? It would take him thousands of years. But already the herald knows his days are numbered. Although he doesn't stop, doesn't rest for even one second, he already knows his undertaking is doomed.

We lay there, thinking and listening to Papa snore-gasping three rooms over. He sounded like an earwig looks under a microscope. I rolled onto my side and nuzzled forward into my big brother's thin arms. He ran his fingers through my hair, whispering, *heart of my heart, heart of my heart,* until I no longer felt scared, and then he said:

—Listen. I have something to show you.

He slipped out of bed, lit the oil lamp on my desk, and asked me where I kept the dolls I no longer loved. I told him they lived under my bed in Papa's old dented leather suitcase. He extracted a fretsaw from one pocket of his robe, a small jar of glue from the other. I propped myself up on the pillows and watched. He sawed off my dolls' legs, hands, and heads, and glued them back in all the wrong places. Legs where arms should be. Six hands trailing along a wooden spine. A head growing out of a belly.

After a while, he invited me to join him. I scrambled down, taking my position cross-legged beside him in my nightie. Soon we were giggling, careful not to wake our parents, constructing our very own oddities exhibition until the black rectangle of my window began graybluing into dawn.

When Gregor tucked me in again, it struck me I hadn't thought about my raw throat and runny nose for hours.

—Have fun today, he said, checking my forehead for a temperature with the back of his hand. And Grete? If the herald doesn't show up? Pretend he doesn't exist. Because you see: in that case it doesn't really matter whether he does or not, does it?

Then I am galloping up the staircase and flying into our flat, kicking off my shoes and unbuttoning my coat as I go.

At the end of the hallway stand Anna and the cook, backs to me. They are peering into the living room. I call to them, but neither responds. I call a second time, louder. The cook turns. A skinny shoot of asparagus, she seems much smaller than she did yesterday. If we stood face-to-face, the top of her dust-colored head would barely reach my breastbone.

Her chafed right hand covers most of her pointy nose and hollow cheeks. Her eyes are open very wide. It takes me a pulse to figure out that the word for what she is doing is *gaping*.

Yes, that is how to say it: the cook is gaping at what she sees.

the chief clerk

It appears there is no one in the fellow's room, that it has been empty all along, that one wing of the door has somehow simply swung open by itself and I have been the brunt of some remarkably distasteful joke—until a vinegary whiff of stale sheets and perspiration reaches me, and I make out, nearly two meters off the floor, a dim bluish-white wedge bobbing in the blackness, and *Oh!* I say, *Oh!* because it is, it comes to me in gradations, a human head, and the human head is peeking at me around the shut wing, which apparition causes a short hiatus in the movement of the universe, and next the rest of a lanky naked body unfolds below it, possessing the sort of physique that well into its thirties might with good reason cause patrons on a beach to mistake it for a gawky teenager's, bony chest narrow as its bony waist, undersized manhood shriveled among a moss of dark blond curls, and my hand, it dawns on me, is at my mouth, my feet backing me away, my retreat feeling as if some steady invisible pressure were driving at me, a wind, an angry spirit, when from my left comes a clomp, and, turning instinctively, I see the old oaf's wife, hair undone and spearing out willy-nilly, sprawling on the floor, robe up around her waist, belt loose, chin on bare freckled chest, cumbersome dugs and hairy privates hideously exposed, and *what's the meaning of this,* I say, *what's the—*

the cook

Wouldn't you know it: moment I sets this evening's thick soup to fart and flabber in its pot, gives the ingredients a chance to get to know each other whilst I turns my attention to serving up breakfast, Anna flutters in in one of her flaps.

—Hurry, ma'am! she cries. *Hurry!* Gregor's terribly ill and can't open his door and Grete is fetching the doctor and the chief clerk is storming around the living room fit to be tied!

I give her one of my long silent stares.

—The eggs is getting cold, I says.

—But, ma'am, she says, the . . .

—Eggs and sausages.

—But, *ma'am* . . .

—Breakfast, lovey, is just this side of ruin.

I wait two shakes before I adds:

—No thanks to *you*.

—But there're the strangest sounds coming from his room and the missus is having one of her visits and the neighbors are starting to poke their heads into the hallway to have a look and listen and . . .

—And you decide to take a quick ten to nose out the latest whisper?

She looks knocked for six.

—No, I . . .

Youth. Always running about like they's three sheets to the wind and none the richer. Can't find their arses with both hands.

—Where on earth did you get off to, then? I says.

Anna huffs a little Anna huff.

—That's . . . *that's* what I'm trying to tell you, ma'am. The master sent me for a locksmith, only I got halfway down the stairs and thought better of going before I told you where I was off to because I . . .

—A locksmith?

—They can't get his door open. He's too sick to even get up.

—You wouldn't be giving me a little leg now, would you?

She looks slapped.

—I swear blind, ma'am!

—Now don't start getting lippy with *me,* I says, thinking meself some thoughts.

I give her a once over, like I'm surrendering at last, though truth is I'm near as curious as her.

—Very well, says I. Very well. Let's have ourselves a look-see.

I wipes me hands on a dishrag, leads the way out of the kitchen, and walks almost smack into the chief clerk nipping past me, bumbleclumping down the stairs. He fetches up a second with his chin on the banisters to take one last glance and, *poof,* he's gone.

Old cow with the smeared lipstick what makes her look like a jester in the rain hawks after him from her open flat door. She turns and hawks me. I gives her a bit of the hawk right back, only twice as sour.

An angry flurry, and her head evaporates.

In the living room I come upon the queerest scene. There the missus is, swaying all at sea in front of the breakfast table, belt untied and robe flapped open, boasting quite a stretch more of the down below than any lady's got a strict right to. Coffee pot behind her's toppled over, last of the brew trickling onto the carpet. Window's wide open as well, rain and cold blowing through like Beelzebub hisself popped round for a stop-by. Going to take Anna and me the rest of the bloody day to clean it up.

And then there's the master, face bloated red and sweaty as a pound of fresh entrails. Got the umbrella the chief clerk left behind in one hand and a rolled-up soggy newspaper in the other and he's waving both over his head like he's conducting a band that ain't paying him no never mind. Busy stamping his feet, too, doing a mad jig, trying to force that bare-assed halfwit of his son back into his room.

—Shoo! the master's yelling. Shoo! Shoo! Shoo!

This ain't what I was hired for.

That's what I'm thinking.

This ain't it at all.

Mind you, I'm perfectly willing to cook breakfast, lunch, and dinner for that outfit. Willing to tidy afterwards. Even willing to clean the odd window, brush the odd hat, push comes to shove.

But this horseshite?

Not an earthly, lovey.

Keeping one eye on his da, the boy starts backing up, takes a bit of a rest, starts backing up some more, takes a bit of a rest. Turns as he goes, slow and wide and jittery, like he can't quite summon up how his arms and legs are supposed to get on with each other.

And that's when the master sees his opening. Steps forward quick as lightning, sets his large right foot on his son's rump, and gives him a mighty shove forward, propelling the lad deep into the darkness beyond. Drops his umbrella and newspaper, reaches out, and slams the door behind him.

Watching him all hunched over there in his robe, panting and wheezing and wheezing and panting, everybody waits for somebody else to say something.

Everybody waits some more.

grete

Our family inhabits the rest of the day like a traveling sales-man in the first instants of waking up in a foreign hotel in a foreign town, unable to place himself. A giant packs our rooms with wool. Papa sits in his armchair near the dining table, wrinkled newspaper winged open in his lap, cold damp wash-cloth palmed over his furry heart. Mutti retreats into her bed-room. She won't come out. Lunchtime approaches and recedes. I stroll down the hall and stand outside her door. I ask if I can come in. She won't answer me.

At twilight I visit the kitchen. The cook perches broom-backed and empty-faced in a chair by the stove. Across from her on a stool, Anna studies her fingernails. She doesn't take her eyes off them even after I ask the cook to pour me a bowl of milk and warm it on the stove. I take a fistful of white bread from a loaf on the counter, tear it into small sops, and sprinkle it in, then carry the concoction to Gregor's door on a tray with a folded napkin and spoon.

I knock, hang back a few seconds before opening up, then slip the bowl inside and withdraw. An hour later I return to re-trieve it. It hasn't been touched. No. That isn't quite true. Gregor has lifted out three soggy nuggets with his fingers and plocked them next to the bowl, on the floorboards at the edge of the carpet.

But he *loves* milk. Milk and bread and cheese. He doesn't eat red meat, despite Papa's badgering. He doesn't smoke, drink, or enjoy sweets like I do. But he *loves* milk. He maintains the diet of an Eastern holy man. He brought it back with him from the war. Fruit. Vegetables. Yogurt. Nuts. Bread. Cheese. Once he caught me nibbling from a bag of chocolates on a bench in the town square. He told me a lemon would probably be better for my system. A lemon! And Gregor thin as a pencil.

Kneeling inside his door, gathering up the spilled sops with the napkin, I steal a glance around. He has moved his chair from his desk to the window and taken a seat there. Still undressed, he is scratching his belly, watching the rain.

In the last gray light of the gray day, I make out the butter-yellow blisters. His shingles are back.

—Gregor, I say. Gregor? Would you like me to get you something else to eat?

A bruise stains his right shoulder where Papa drove him through the door. The way his hair sticks out all over makes it seem he is hanging upside down in an upside-down room. I wonder what a doctor could do for him now.

—Everyone is worried about you, I say.

His bed remains unmade, his sofa cocked away from the wall. A collection of cloth samples and open fashion magazines are laid out across his desk. On top lie his fretsaw and a pair of scissors.

—Tell us what we did, I say.

On the flowered wallpaper above his desk hangs a photograph he must have snipped from one of the magazines and set in a gilt frame. It wasn't there yesterday. A Scandinavian model wearing nothing but a fur cap, fur stole, and huge fur muff into which her forearm has disappeared poses on a white box against a white background.

Her lips are so nastily red they send a shudder through me.

It smells funny in here, dense, like unaired bedding and divans used by old people. I rise, balancing the bowl in the middle of the tray. I wait to see if my big brother will turn to check if I'm still standing here.

He doesn't.

After a while, I give up and withdraw.

Mutti doesn't come out for dinner. I can tell from the crack at the bottom of her door that she hasn't lit her lamp. It is just Papa and me at the table in a room that the giant has stuffed with wool. We sip our chicken soup and gaze straight ahead and can't think of anything to say.

Anna serves us, removing the empty bowls without a word when we're done. Her face is as unfilled with expression as a ladle of cold porridge. She seems uncomfortable, unused to all this stillness around her. When she reaches for my glass of water, to refill it, I notice her hand is shaking. I pretend I don't see and thank her. That only makes her hand shake more.

Two loud clunks come from Gregor's room, one right after the other. The water pitcher rattles down on the table, but it doesn't tip over because Anna is still gripping the handle. I imagine my big brother rising, pushing his chair aside, and running headfirst into the wall.

Papa stops in mid-sip, lowers his spoon, and looks at me with his sad eyes.

I stop eating, too.

I dab my mouth with my napkin, push back from the table, excuse myself. Willing my mind vacant, I cross to Gregor's door, open it a crack, feel around inside until I locate the key, extract it and bring it around to our side.

Then I return to the table and continue dining.

the servant girl

I lie here in the wee hours, the cook twitching in her sleep beside me under our quilt, scaring myself with what he might be doing in there.

It must be three o'clock. Another hour and a half and I have to get up to start lending a hand with breakfast. I roll onto my tummy, pull the pillow over my head, and imagine my new shoes in the store window.

It doesn't help.

I can still hear him scrabbling around, restless, gibbering.

Just when I think maybe he has given up, finally tired himself out and fallen asleep, the scuffing begins. It sounds as if he is rubbing his head back and forth against the door. As if he wants to get out.

And I have to piddle.

I didn't have to a minute ago, but now I do.

I think I can hold it until morning and then I think I can't. I don't want to reach under the bed for the chamber pot. I hold it and hold it, and then I can't hold it anymore. I give up and take care of business. It isn't as bad as I thought.

Careful not to disturb the cook, I slip out from beneath the covers, tidy up at the washstand, put on my clothes, and tiptoe through the flat toward Grete's door. The hallway is longer at night than during the day. It has more turns. My shoulder jabs a doorjamb. It feels like I am making my way through a warren. I think about all the things living in here with me.

After what seems a very long time, I reach her door. I knock. She answers immediately. She must have been having trouble sleeping, too.

—I'd like to stay in the kitchen from now on, miss, I say, rubbing my shoulder.

Grete examines me with those eyes they have.

—You mean at night? she asks. You already sleep off the kitchen.

—Night and day, miss. With the door locked, miss.

She opens her mouth to argue with me, closes it without saying anything, and then opens it and says:

—Fine.

—I shall unlock it only on special summons.

She looks at my hand rubbing my shoulder. My hand stops. I have never done something like this before. Examining me, she asks:

—Is there anything else?

—No, miss, I say.

—Good. Go back to bed.

And she shuts the door in my face.

margaret

The woman who last night dreamed of wrestling Franz Kafka in her bathtub walks up New Oxford Street through sparkling bluegray morning light, turns left at Bloomsbury Street and right at Great Russell, passes the young soldier selling old war ribbons from a cart, and mounts the steps of the British Museum in a great swirl of pigeons.

She takes her place in the security line before the metal detectors in the main hall and touches her hand to her black hair cropped short like Julius Caesar's, then straightens her black cateye glasses that don't need straightening.

Margaret wears a baggy black sweater, tight black jeans, black sneakers, and black socks. She saw a bright yellow poster for a book club above the mailboxes yesterday on her way home from work and straightaway decided to go. It will convene at nine o'clock this evening at a pub called the World's End around the corner from her flat in Camden Town. While she took out a copy of the novella from the Camden Town public library this morning, Margaret prefers to enjoy it in the reading room of the British Museum because the reading room's dome and dark wood and gilt and hush and sense of dignified industry remind her of an England she can't quite believe ever existed.

She is tired of her own scruffy neighborhood. She has lived there longer than she has lived anywhere else since leaving home. Her job consists of selling people shoes they may not want to buy at one of the cluttered shops indistinguishable from all the other cluttered shops lining Camden High Street. Joining a book club is consistent with her plan to meet people other than her naff colleagues. They have never heard of Kafka and couldn't carry on a conversation with her about anything even mildly noteworthy if their voluminous pants sagging halfway down their arses depended on it.

Margaret majored in studio art at the poly on the grounds that she had sort of liked to draw when she was a little girl. She read several of Kafka's short stories for her lit class. The professor, a skinny nervous man in his late twenties who shaved his head and dressed like a DJ, adored Kafka. Margaret remembers how he paced back and forth, a natty toy duck in a shooting gallery, and employed his hands above his head to tell the lecture hall about how the Czech author wrote what he considered his first successful story in a single autumn night when he was already almost thirty years old. And how, on the heels of that, in three short weeks, he wrote a mysterious parable about a man who awoke one day as an insect. The more you studied that story, the natty toy duck said, the less you understood it.

That plus a few short pieces of fiction and a review or two were all Kafka ever published before he died at forty-one of tuberculosis. Toward the end, the lesions on his larynx prevented him from speaking or swallowing. He penned one-line poemnotes to the people around him while starving to death.

Believing his writing life had been a failure, in one of those poem-notes he asked his best friend, Max Brod, to burn all his unpublished manuscripts. After three years of soul-searching, his best friend complied.

Margaret finds this all quite grim. She remembers her professor pacing back and forth and employing his hands above his head to tell the lecture hall that the amazing thing about what

Kafka wrote is how it always seems to *almost* make sense, but not quite. Like sacred texts, he said. She wrote in her notebook, which she still has around somewhere: *Kafka's fiction appears to exist in order to be misinterpreted.*

But what she remembers most is how, in one of the stories she dipped into while working on her class essay, she came across a brief description of the Statue of Liberty holding a sword instead of a torch, and how the gleaming bridge in the background connected Manhattan to Boston instead of New Jersey. She loved how strange that made her feel, as if she could sense the pressure of another world pushing against the membrane of this one so hard she could distinguish its outlines poking through.

Margaret isn't very keen on reading. Not as a rule, at any rate. Reading usually makes her feel unsettled and distracted. When the urge does strike her, she drops into the Camden Town public library and follows interesting-looking people as they browse the stacks, taking note of what books they choose, waiting for them to go away, and then picking one on either side of the empty slot they leave behind. The first sentence is usually enough for her to make a decision because the first sentence almost always holds the entire book in miniature within it. If that does the trick, she continues through the first paragraph, the first page, the first chapter.

If things begin turning stodgy, too predictable, or too complicated, Margaret feels no compunction about putting the book on a nearby table and simply walking away.

And now here she stands in the main hall of the British Museum, *The Metamorphosis* in the young corpulent fingers of the young corpulent security guard sorting through her backpack.

—Good read, innit? he asks her.

Margaret looks up at him. She has been thinking of other things. Without altering her expression, she replies:

—I'll let you know.

Smiling to himself, the security guard returns the book to her backpack, snaps shut the flap, and without meeting her eyes returns it with one hand while signaling for the next person in line to step forward.

Shrugging her pack over her right shoulder, which Margaret awoke to find achy this morning, she returns to worrying about her grandparents, Neddie and Nellie. Two weeks ago they went missing near their home in Yorkshire. They are admirably sprightly and sociable people for being in their early eighties, always part of community dances and chatty evenings at the local pub. Friday they were supposed to go to a party hosted by their friends, Tim and Shirley, but they never appeared. The following day Shirley rang them up to see if everything was all right. When no one answered, she popped around to discover the front door to Neddie and Nellie's cottage unlocked, the cottage itself in perfect order, the garage empty. She phoned Tim. Tim phoned the police. The police launched a search.

Margaret fears that, even though they lived in the same place their entire married lives, running a small café in Haworth until retiring twenty years ago, Neddie and Nellie, getting on as they are, might have gotten lost on the desolate roads meandering through the moors and had some kind of dreadful accident.

On her way up the stairs to the reading room, she recalls how she played for hours every day during her autumn holidays in the spooky, bleak, rusty landscape behind Neddie and Nellie's cottage before being called in for scones and a cup of Earl Grey. There were no other kids, no other houses, in any direction. It made Margaret feel like a tiny astronaut all alone on a faraway planet.

Margaret loved that sensation the same way she did Kafka's description of the Statue of Liberty.

It made her feel special, focused, free to let anything happen.

A tall man in a smart blue business suit rushes down the stairs Margaret is trying to walk up and inadvertently catches her elbow with his umbrella, jerking her sideways as he passes.

—Sorry, he says over his shoulder, clippity-clopping into the future chased by something no one else can see.

Margaret has wrestled Franz Kafka before in her dreams. Sometimes sinking in the brown slop of a Scottish bog. Sometimes jammed in the loo of a 747 jetting five miles above a stormy Atlantic on its way to New York. Sometimes leaning against the kitchen counter in her Camden Town flat, back to her broken Sanyo toaster oven, pong of sour milk in the air, little mice with elongated human faces skittering around her feet.

—*Heart of my heart,* Franz Kafka whispers in her ear while he strangles her. *Heart of my heart.*

grete

Next morning I visit the kitchen again. I am in my nightgown. Mutti and Papa are still asleep, the cook and servant girl just beginning to stir next door. One of them splashes at the wash-stand, tiny bird in a park fountain.

I pick out Papa's soggy newspaper from the trash, spread it open on the counter, collect a large selection of food to put in it. Perhaps I can figure out what Gregor wants to eat. A dollop of yogurt. A handful of almonds. A few raisins. A buttered roll and chunk of bread. A small sliver of bland white cheese.

Wrapping it up like a fish at the market, I am struck by another idea. I unwrap it again and add a few wilted leaves of cabbage and a large bone from several set aside for this evening's soup. It is covered with creamy yellow fat.

I can't find Gregor anywhere in his room. The chair he was sitting in last night is on its side on the floor. I set his meal on the newspaper inside the door, then loiter, squinting into the fusty dimness, listening. Gregor always used to be so hard to please. No suit was ever pressed as well as it might have been; no vegetables cooked to his satisfaction. And here I am setting out these leftovers on a newspaper for him to pick through like a beggar. Sometimes moments arrive in winces.

Last week Mutti, who can never keep a secret, told me my big brother planned to make an important announcement at Christmas. He was going to say that, despite the expense involved, he intended to send me to the Conservatorium next year to study the violin. He felt my studies would benefit not only myself, but the entire family. Someday I might even be able to join the symphony and make a passable income.

I planned to tell him no.

Thank you, but no.

Gregor believes I have potential, but I am one of those very good musicians who will never be among those very excellent ones. My problem is this: I have to contemplate rather than feel when I play. The outcome is something contrived. I know it will not change no matter how many lessons I take or how much I practice.

It used to hurt, knowing such a thing, only now I understand this is how I am put together. Growing up is a process of losing things. My big brother believes the contrary for no other reason than that he is my big brother. His money would be better spent on our family's other needs. Mutti should see a doctor about her asthma. Papa shouldn't have to work at his age. Our family should be able to live in a flat suitable to our standing.

A rustling from beneath the sofa, and I glance over to see it cocked farther from the wall than it was last night. The sheet from Gregor's bed has been stripped off and draped over it. Something bulbs out the cloth near the floorboards. I have to stare in the half-light before realizing it is his head. He has shinnied under there. He must have seen my reaction yesterday evening and taken it upon himself to spare me the sight of him. Yet all of him can't quite fit. A bare foot sticks out the far end, toes curled.

—I thought you might like some food, I say. You haven't eaten since the day before yesterday. You must be famished.

I go over and kneel down, raise the sheet, have a closer look. Gregor can't lift his head. It is wedged in sideways. His eyes are shut as if, by not seeing me, he can will me somewhere else. Above his left eyebrow rises a discolored lump from where he ran into the wall. His face is burgundy, the veins on his forehead bulging like fleshy worms. He is holding his breath, attempting to force himself to faint until I go away.

Letting down the sheet again, I say:

—It's okay. I won't look. I'll tidy things a bit while you rest, then be on my way.

I stand and open the window to let in some fresh air. Make his bed without the sheet, right his chair, dust a little with the hem of my nightgown around the commotion on his desk. Done, I close the window. As I turn to leave, a voice both his and not his commences speaking.

There is a girlish pitch to it. Its ramble reminds me of a bicycle clattering down a bumpy hill without brakes.

—But if I'm late again, it is saying to itself, but if I'm late, there are so many doors in this house, I don't know why, and so we ran across the pasture at night, we boys, and the last thing I wanted was to look back, look behind me into blackness, because if I'm late, you see, Papa will lock me outside on the balcony again, and all I want to do is lie here in this boat and close my eyes and feel the air breathing across me, the waves rocking, because you can try, you can try and try, but in the end the train sometimes simply doesn't show up . . .

—You won't be late, I say.

I am still at the window. The room is lightening. When we were children, I sometimes snuck into his room and watched him sleep. The expression on his face suggested the dream he was having was explaining everything to him.

Several blocks away, the trams have started up.

—Because the boys, you see, because of them, as if I could

think of the words, because if you miss it everybody will slow down, and then the colors will start again, except once I wished for peace on earth, and everyone on the planet disappeared.

—I brought you some breakfast.

—Count them, go on, except I look at my watch and then they are shouting *Come down! Come down! Come down!* just like that, *bam,* into the wall, *bam,* where did the time go, I know it's under here somewhere, would you please help me look . . .

I move toward the door, but already I am back in my room, dressed, down the stairs, hurrying along the rainy street with my coat collar clinched against the bluster. I don't know where I am going. It doesn't matter. I close my eyes. I see a circus.

High up in the crimson tent two trapeze artists performing.

One hanging by his long blond hair from the teeth of the other.

Then the first one opens his mouth to sing, and the second drops away.

ραρα

—You aren't doing half badly with him, The Father declares, settling into his easy chair.

He parts the top half of his robe, applies his washcloth to his heart, and, pressing back into the soft fabric, exhales. The far shore of the day always approaches as a kind of blessing, there having been so many worries to swim through to reach it. Once upon a time, The Father assumed his golden years would consist of an extended unclenching, but that time feels very long ago as, through partially closed eyelids, he watches his daughter add a fresh shovelful of coal to the stove, damp it down, and move to the dining table to sit near her mother.

His daughter reminds him of someone. He can't quite place it, but she reminds him of someone he used to know. Trying to recall, he asks her to fetch him a beer.

The Father's wife is working on her needlepoint: something congested with pink roses and green leaves. He believes he can pick out a tint of, if not happiness, then acceptance in her features. He is relieved. It has been difficult for her. She has taken it harder than the rest. When young, she was strong and brisk and determined. Recently she has become more delicate, more prone to a certain nervousness about being alive.

Grete returns, bringing with her a gust of tart fumes from the stove, followed by the servant girl carrying The Father's beer. He lifts it off the tray without acknowledging her presence, swigs a sugary barley mouthful, and puts down the mug on the side table. He waits for the servant girl to leave and his daughter to take her seat before, head back, taking satisfaction in the way the washcloth's coolness radiates from the core of his being outward, a creeping azure glow, he says:

—I had my doubts, but you aren't doing half badly at all.

Looking down at her hands flat on the tabletop, Grete says:

—Thank you, Papa.

—Isn't it lovely having an evening in like this with family? Mutti pipes up. I can't imagine anywhere I'd rather be.

She adjusts her paper pattern and contemplates it.

Through partially closed eyelids, The Father watches Grete reach for her violin and prepare to play, and he feels the carp of a question well up from deep down inside him, sees it rising out of the watery obscurity.

—But don't you sometimes find yourself wondering, he listens to himself asking, whether or not, strictly speaking, he is your brother?

Grete puts down her violin.

—Given the circumstances, I mean, he adds.

—Because, says The Father's wife, paying The Father no heed, more than enough is sometimes too much. Yet what we have here is just right, don't you think? Did you hear what happened to Mrs. Klinghoffer last week? Such a story!

Mrs. Klinghoffer is the next-door neighbor who won't mind her own business. Her husband, an agreeable balding chap whose bad teeth appeared to be speckled with caramel, was killed three years ago on the front. A captain in the cavalry, he had his throat slit while sleeping in his tent. Some said it was an enemy assassin, others his own men tired and frightened of being where they were. He and The Father used to exchange pleasantries on the stairs. He was always decked out in his dress uniform.

The Father wouldn't be entirely surprised to learn, upon her own passing, that Mrs. Klinghoffer was a Jewess. What other race, after all, he wonders, could overdo the cosmetics and trinkets like that, making their faces the orange, yellow, and green of a Matisse, sporting fistfuls of jewelry for a quick trip to the vegetable vender? In any event, her wiry hair was undeniably reddish in hue.

—It's a trivial affair, The Father goes on. Hardly worth mentioning, really. But I simply find myself speculating about it from time to time.

Grete stares at her hands.

—She was seen at the fishmonger's in her slippers, Mutti says. It appears she left her flat in such a rush she forgot to change into her good shoes. Did you ever!

She laughs merrily.

—If our son loved us, you see, The Father explains, I suppose the question would fail to present itself. Appreciated all we've done for him and so forth. As it is, one can't help asking, can one? It's just a thought. He's always been the leg-puller. Didn't we all once assume we could count on him to take care of your mother and me in our old age? That we could rely on his fortitude and wherewithal? He said as much upon several occasions, to the best of my recollection. Such a kidder, that boy.

The Father takes another swig of beer.

—*I* would have been horrified, says The Father's wife. Just think of it! Glancing down at your feet in the town square and seeing a pair of slippers instead of shoes! Oh, dear God in heaven!

She laughs again, and then sound briefly departs the room.

A held breath of seconds, and Grete says something too faintly for The Father to hear. He doesn't ask her to repeat herself because, sliding toward a luxurious doze, he remembers now. It comes to him like a myoclonic jerk. How he rang up his wife, just as in a bad movie, to say he was having dinner with a buyer, when in fact he was having dinner with the buyer's daughter. A businesswoman in her early twenties, she wore plum lipstick and a pleated skirt with a snug blouse and collar of white, fine-meshed lace.

And her shoes.

The Father has always been a shoe man.

He could not keep his eyes off those black ones with the bright brass buckles. They made his stomach weak.

If he had to say why he did it, put his finger on the reason, he would have proposed what transpired did so primarily due to the nature of gravity. How, he wanted to say, it operated not unlike a bacterial infection. How the aging skin beneath one's eyes cannot be immunized.

Contrary to what one might expect, The Father and the businesswoman discovered over a fine meal at a restaurant on the far side of the river that they had remarkably much in common. So much so, it began to pain The Father to see how many things they had to talk about. Her dreams were his memories. His desires were her experience.

On the pretense of going over some more numbers, he half-invited himself back to her flat. She did not turn him down. And—again a surprise—they did nothing except talk a little more about commerce, about what they didn't have in common, which is what, in a sense, they did. Not long after the servants had been dismissed for the night, The Father heard himself asking, apropos of nothing, really, an outrageous question.

He heard himself asking if it might be possible for them to hug for a minute or two.

—Nothing else, mind you, The Father added quickly.

He brought up the proposal matter-of-factly, as if he might be discussing a minor modification to her father's company's operations. All he wanted to do, he said, feeling himself blush, was to feel the press of a newer body against his older one. He was sure, at her age, she wouldn't understand, he said, and, naturally, he more than sympathized if she were disinclined, but it had been nothing if not an odd day, and he felt the spontaneous urge to ask, and, well, so ask he did, because . . . because that was simply the kind of man he was.

The Father couldn't believe his own ears. He fully anticipated she would say no, of course, and, as he spoke, the businesswoman stared at him expressionlessly, as if at a shoddily dressed stranger who had stopped her on the street to ask her a question in Latvian.

And then, more surprising still, she said yes.

The Father, who had been sitting across from her, stood, crossed the small space separating them, and joined the young businesswoman on the sofa. In a series of awkward moves, he leaned forward and embraced her.

In his mind's eye, they looked like a pair of cousins more than lovers. Closing his eyes, he drew in the lilac fragrance of her perfume. He gave himself over to the sensation of her skin through her snug silk blouse, noting her frame was thin, even bony, more a boy's than a woman's. Her back muscles never fully relaxed, never fully allowed themselves to be a part of this event.

And next, just like that, he disengaged himself and made a show of consulting his watch. Rising, he announced he had to be going. He had to be getting home. He kissed her hand, bowed like a gentleman, and thanked her for a delightful evening in a tone that said no matter what they ever thought of doing together in the future, it would never be this.

Wordless, puzzled, she stood by the sofa, watching him gather his things. He saw himself out and arrived back at his own flat not long past midnight. Standing just inside the bedroom door, The Father listened to his wife sleeping. She was making clacking sounds through her nose. While he would not say that love for her flooded him, exactly, he would say that for some reason he felt extremely good.

He felt he could remain there for a long, long time, doing precisely what he was doing.

That was five years ago.

The next day his life changed with the abruptness of a tram juddering off the rails in rush hour.

Margi.
That was it.
Her name had been Margi.

How pretty.

grete

A long period of inwardness descends upon us. All I can do is glide through the motions that make up the hours, remembering.

When the cook quits, promising Mutti not to tell a soul what she has seen here, I take over in the kitchen. Sometimes Anna can help show me what to do, but it doesn't matter much. No one is hungry. We sit at the table, waiting for each meal to be over, Mutti looking perplexed, as if she has forgotten the name of each item on her plate.

Mornings I whisk through Gregor's door, throw open the window, and stand by it until the odors of exhaled breath and unwashed hair thin out. I straighten up and sweep what remains from yesterday into a bucket that I cover with a wooden lid and take away. Twice a day I feed him—once early, before anyone else is awake, and once after the midday meal, when Mutti and Papa take a long nap and Anna runs errands. Gregor carries leftovers to his chair by the window. He seems to enjoy the diffuse presence of the light.

Occasionally I ask him to tell me the story of the Emperor. He sits in his chair, squinting ahead, his eyes a little less for seeing every day.

I bring him my pair of shiny black high heels and dark dress with the pretty embroidered chrysanthemums on the collar. I slip the dress over his head, squeeze his feet into the shoes. His body is so limp it seems as if a butcher has removed his bones. I apply Chinese-red lipstick to his lips and rouge to his cheeks and tease his hair and step back to admire my work.

He asks, looking past me over my shoulder:

—Are we having an imaginary conversation?

—Yes, I say. We are.

—Because when you are dead you have to stay up all night. Have you perhaps seen what I've done with my hands?

Next morning the dress and high heels are piled beside the remnants of his meal. Gregor is back under the couch. He has smeared the lipstick and rouge across his face.

I reach out to pat what is left of his pretty teased hair and without warning he tilts back and nips the fleshy base of my palm.

I don't think about slapping him. I just slap him. Hard across the top of the head. He flinches and begins talking to himself as though I am no longer in the room. I let him go on for a while, giving him some time to think about what he has done, then ask:

—Do you remember Georg, Gregor? Do you remember what we used to do on Saturday afternoons?

He closes his eyes.

Holds his breath.

I have strong feelings for the person my brother is not.

We played dress-up. Gregor and I were fond enough of putting on our parents' clothes, but it was Georg who loved our costume parties more than anything in the world. To step into Mutti's pumps, wear my clothes, wrap himself in a primrose taffeta boa—nothing could make him happier.

His passion led him to design the costume he wore as a hunger artist: black tights, black sock-boots, wide black belt. I helped powder his face white; Gregor shaved his head. Georg was so thin his ribs rimpled out. He looked like an underfed creature that had crawled from the center of the earth into the sun for the first time.

In those days there were many hunger artists, but my brother was the best in the province. People knew which cage in the square was his. They would even show up at night to watch him lying on the straw floor in the flickering torchlight. Children stood open-mouthed, holding hands. Adults crossed themselves. Sometimes Georg took a sip of water from a tiny glass to moisten his lips, or stretched an arm through the bars so people could feel how scraggy it was, and they would applaud. Mostly, though, he sat quietly while the onlookers admired his work and dropped coins at his feet.

The town hired relays of permanent observers to monitor him, although everyone knew Georg would never stoop to cheating. Other hunger artists might sneak a digestive biscuit, a handful of raisins hidden beneath the straw, but never Georg. Fasting came naturally to him. He treasured its athleticism.

There was great fanfare when his cage was opened at the end of a performance. An observer slipped in to examine him. Once Georg had been pronounced fit, two pigtailed girls chosen by lottery helped him out to a table piled high with grilled meats, bananas, strawberries, breads, and bushy vegetables. That is how Georg broke his fast. What no one except Gregor and I knew was that it was also the only really difficult part for him. Georg despised having to eat in public. The notion of such filth entering his body in front of a large audience appalled him.

I don't know why skilled fasting fell out of favor. Fans began losing interest. Maybe many preferred staying home, listening to adventure shows on the radio, or attending the increasingly flashy acts that had started coming through town. The old man who threw punches at himself until he collapsed in a bloody heap. The miniature bearded fat lady in the rose-tan sequined tutu who cried out each time she breathed fire from her nose.

One day, a reviewer in the local paper proclaimed hunger artistry dead, and most people believed him. Of course, Georg knew better. He recognized his undertaking had been nothing if not a way to help others see things they might not otherwise have seen. But people were growing tired of having to work so hard.

The less they cared about what he did, the more zealous Georg became. That is how he left us. One autumn afternoon he set up his cage at the base of the giant clock in the square and entered what he declared would be his greatest performance yet.

The first forty days came and went swiftly.

Then sixty.

Seventy-five.

Although almost no one came to watch for fun anymore except for Gregor and me, Georg didn't stop until the hundredth morning of the hundredth day—far beyond the record set by any hunger artist in our province—when one of the permanent observers noticed that Georg, who had crawled under the straw to stay warm for the night, wasn't moving.

Twenty minutes later, Mutti's lungs failed. Gregor stopped talking for two weeks. Papa railed and railed against my dead brother.

—What a fool he was, he said. What a bloody stupid way to die.

He promised he would never utter his son's name again in our house, and he kept his word.

Sometimes, after we had helped him dress up on Saturday afternoons, Georg would reward us by showing us sketches of his favorite insects in the book he kept beneath the sofa in the living room. There were pretty butterflies that lived by drinking juices from dead animals. Wasps whose larvae would chew their way out of the caterpillars in whose bodies the adults had laid their eggs. But Georg always returned to the scarab beetles. I don't think it was the dome of dark brown belly that attracted him to them, the glass-drop bulbs at the ends of their antennae, or the tiny chocolate blisters of their blank shelled eyes. I think it was how, inside all that ugliness, there existed a pair of flimsy wings concealed beneath the hard cover of their backs. Expanded, those wings could carry the beetles for miles and miles in a blundering flight.

The even odder thing, though, was how during their entire lifetimes the beetles seldom, if ever, used them.

It was as if they had forgotten they were even there.

Guilty, I decide to spend the rest of the morning on a visit to the baker for some day-old bread to make things right with Gregor.

The rain has come down so violently so long it has forced the rats out of the sewers. I have to veer around smoldering hip-high pyres of their carcasses to make my way along the pavement. The stench of burning fur is everywhere. I hold my lace kerchief over my nose.

In place of the downpour, a heavy silver smog has settled over the city. It turns everything into a glary photograph that hasn't been fully developed. The impression is that reality's corners have been erased, that light always has the last word.

Even though I have lived here my entire life, assume I have every lane committed to memory, I take two corners and don't know where I am. Usually I orient myself by sighting half a block ahead of me. Now I can't see more than a meter. I find myself in alleys I thought were avenues, avenues I thought were other avenues.

Just as I am about to give up, I round a corner and there squats the bakery. The proprietor is a huge neckless man with patches of irritated skin across his bald head. He does not look especially startled by my request, not even when I ask him for day-old pastries to go along with the day-old bread. He disappears briefly and returns with several forms to fill out. One is three pages long. I look at them, at him.

—I don't understand, I say.

—New paperwork from the city council.

—May I ask what for?

—They tell me to hand it out to anyone asking for day-old products. I hand it out. This is what I know.

—All the bakeries in town are doing this?

He shrugs and watches the forms on the counter as if they might do something interesting. I consider my options, then lean over and fill them out. They are not as complicated as they at first appear, but they ask many more questions than one might think germane to issues of buying day-old bakery goods.

The clerk disappears again and this time returns with a large white paper bag filled with my purchase. I pay and leave without saying thank you, stepping from the shop directly into the path of a passerby. We collide. It is a lieutenant with black hair combed straight back, a short well-trimmed beard, the scent of limes tangy around him.

—Ah! he says. *Terribly* sorry! Are you all right?

—It's completely my fault. What a perfect scatterbrain I must be today. I . . .

—Nonsense. You absolutely must accept my apology. Otherwise I won't take another step. I shall remain standing on this square of earth until Doomsday. Is this what you'd like weighing on your conscience?

I feel myself smile, smile and blush, wondering what I am thinking, and it comes to me that this is how certain important things commence.

herrmann

Reminds me a bit of a cricket, really, what with the wedge-shaped face and broomstick legs. But any port in a storm, lad, any port in a storm. Turn on the old charm. Invite her to the café. Nowhere to be for an hour or two.

Can't very well play a game she doesn't know the rules to, can she. It's the uniform. Uniform and wit and boyish smile. Irresistible mixture of urbanity and vulnerability. Not an achievement to be sniffed at in this jaded day and age.

I do most of the talking up front, naturally. Make her feel comfortable. Comment on the atrocious weather, strolling past storefronts, large low airship whirring through the fog above us.

Inside the coffee-tanged muggy warmth, I make sure everything appears to change from my court to hers. Help her off with the overcoat. Pull out the chair. Order for us both over the espresso machine's steamy hiss.

Name's Grete, and Grete tries to put on the prissy missy for me. Frightfully out of her league. Her hobbies apparently consist of pouting and feeling martyred. Simplest way to her heart is the art of feigned attentiveness. Smooth your face. Lean forward. Meet her eyes. The rest is simply daydreaming and reeling in the minutes.

Takes me back to that boy I chatted up in the St. Petersburg bar last spring because he wore his white satin shirt unbuttoned all the way down to his navel. Thought he knew what was what. Thought he'd been around the block. They all do.

By the time he picked up the right station it was next morning and he was well and truly fucked, lying all alone in his fleabag bed while yours truly had taken the liberty of divesting a fiver from his breeches before leaving.

I try to conjure up his name, then recall I never knew it, then begin wondering what's going on beneath that nice blouse of the cricket before me.

Catch sight over her shoulder of four shites with shaved heads, black shirts, and black boots talking noisily in back: local worker bees for the White Resistance. Bet you a week's pay they're in it for the spiffy look. Hatred always being a fashion statement at the end of the day.

If I weren't otherwise engaged, I'd fetch a few mates around for a bit of fun when they stepped out for a piss in the mews.

Afraid I'm committed to hearing The Family Tragedy instead. Chap can find one behind every woman in a nice camelhair overcoat. This one's outright operatic. Brave brother fighting up on the front. Stalwart Pater wounded in the Burmese jungle, currently limping through life on a wooden peg. Mater, due to the aforementioned, soft around the trauma.

I reach out and pat Grete's wrist tenderly, mostly to shut her up:

—It must have been an absolute horror for you.

She's on the verge of tears. Shakes her head to clear it of her existence and looks quite pretty for a moment, then laughs and doesn't.

—Enough about me, she says. Your ears must be smarting. Tell me about yourself. I can't begin to imagine what it must be like out there.

—Oh, well, nothing much to say about it, really. Sounds rather like a swarm of metal flies bouncing off the tin roofs around you, the bullets do, when you're in the thick of it. I was up on tour when they were building those roads that led nowhere to confuse our boys. Had the gall to lounge about, drinking their execrable tea and smoking their hubble-bubbles, waiting for us to show up so they could snipe us off one at a time. You'd be walking along some godforsaken trail of rubble when suddenly the fellow beside you would sit down with this flummoxed look on his face, and you'd realize he was no longer in possession of his right forearm . . .

Cricket becomes a shrinking violet.

—Sorry, I say. Sorry. I didn't mean to . . .

—How in the world does one get through it? I should think one would want to curl up in a corner and wait for it all to be over.

—Contrary to the chestnut, it's not so much like wandering through a bad dream as it is being very, very awake at two in the morning. Home's the place that feels dreamlike after a month or two.

I take my last mouthful of coffee, signal the cute blond waiter with the tight trousers for the bill.

—Fancy a stroll? I ask, turning back. I don't mean to be forward, but I'd be honored to accompany you.

She blushes again.

Very good at that sort of thing.

—I couldn't possibly inconvenience you.

—If this constitutes inconvenience, please do bring on the fleet of it. I dab my beard with my napkin, lower my head in mock anticipation, give her a sweet grin. Deal?

—Deal.

—Brilliant!

I pay, help her on with her overcoat, offer to carry her bright white package, offer her my arm, and off we amble.

And that's that, really. That's the show.

Because she is mine now, you see.

mutti

You think your life — during the day that is — you think it can work — but your body kicks you out of your sleep — to remind you of the opposite — Papa snoring beside you — reassuring berm of noise — ghost rinsing out your heart with soda water — and all you can see — lying here in the darkness — all you can think about at this hour — are the stories the neighbors must be telling each other — or maybe — Lord willing — maybe they've already begun forgetting you had a son in the first place — gradually that is — in the fullness of time — maybe that's why the Lord invented defective memory — way of letting the misfortunes go — but here you are — smack in the middle of them — you know you should be preparing for Christmas — tree decorations food cards — the flat too large by half — but you can't leave it — can't move — not with him about — or maybe — yes — in some sort of box — wooden with breathing holes — Papa could drill them — hard to lift — all that pointing in the street — still — it could be done — in the abstract — explain we're merely moving lodgings — carrying our belongings from one to the next — unless he becomes restless inside — begins his jabbering — or the thing slipped — slipped and fell and broke open — oh dear God in heaven — huge wooden egg splintering in the street — him spilling naked onto the cobblestones — the idea too much to bear — we can always rent out a room or two instead — everyone does it these days — stay right where we

are — because Grete tells me — she says she keeps the electric
lights off in there — at night — on foggy days — saves us a
few pfennigs — every one counts — not much need for food
either — reminds me of myself back then — always thinking
of others — and he doesn't seem to mind — difficult to say for
certain — still — how over the course of a lifetime — all the
options — how they funnel down into this one — *pretty as a
picture* they used to say — *look at you* — *your whole life before
you* — then one night you wake up here don't you — never
saw it skidding by — who would have thought — all those
hours of being yourself — stretching out ahead of you — you
reach for Papa's plump rump — pat it reassuringly — a relief to
know it's there — his snore breaks in half — a groggy shifting
— great disturbed walrus — resettling — muttering in his
sleepvoice — *my chin* he says — *my chin* — and sinks under
again — leaving you behind — leaving you with nothing but
yourself again —

the cashier

You raise your chin while counting out change at the milliner's shop and wonder whatever happened to him.

The thought arrives from nowhere the same way you sometimes forget you were supposed to do something yesterday and then you feel uneasy and then you remember. The woman in front of you has on the wrong shade of makeup for her complexion. She stopped applying foundation halfway down her neck and it makes her look like she's wearing someone else's head.

—I don't have all day, you know, she tells you.

—I'm terribly sorry, Mrs. Klinghoffer. I must have been daydreaming. Here you go. One and five makes six. Good morning.

She turns without wishing you a good morning back. The tiny bells on the door jingle crazily behind her, and the shop is empty. You take a seat on your stool behind the counter.

Closing your eyes, you follow him as he entered the shop last summer. You were preparing to hang out the lunch sign when he arrived with what you assumed to be his mousy girlfriend. Her hair a honey frizz. She needed to eat more. They both did. They reminded you of stray cats. Looking at her made you feel a bit better about yourself.

Despite the heat, he wore a light-gray suit with a stiff-collared white shirt, dark tie, matching bowler. His shiny brown eyes burrowed inside you even when they didn't mean to. He seemed embarrassed by their straightforwardness.

—Good day, he said. I believe a hat is ready for my sister. Miss Samsa.

His voice was gentler than most men's. It felt like he had just stroked your cheek.

Going through the boxes on the pickup shelf in back, you wondered how a family could have produced two such different versions of itself, the sister a caricature of her brother. All her features were his features, only out of proportion.

She had chosen the small wheat turban of fancy braid with black erect pile-velvet facing, black satin ribbon trimming around the crown, and fancy black stickup on the side.

Mr. Samsa lifted the hat from the box, rotated it in his hands, and passed it to her.

—Oh, it's *lovely*! she said.

—Try it on.

She did, carefully, as if mimicking a princess, then consulted her reflection in the small mirror on the mahogany stand on the counter. It appeared to you she was wearing a fruit bowl.

—*Very* becoming, you said.

—Happy birthday, said Mr. Samsa.

He paid in cash and they left and you went about your business. You thought about his eyes through the rest of the day but only as if they were hovering at the wrong end of a telescope.

Next morning the tiny bells tinkled and clinked, and he walked through the door alone. He seemed queasy, as though his breakfast hadn't quite agreed with him. When he saw you were the only girl in the shop, he smiled. He was wearing a different suit, elegant acorn brown with matching bowler and tiny red rose on his lapel.

—Mr. Samsa. Is there something I can do for you, sir? I do hope everything's in order with your sister's hat.

—Oh, it's been a tremendous success at home. My sister worships it. My mother believes it's the height of style. My father treats it as he might a meteorite turned up on the breakfast table. But that's my father.

He studied the wooden planks beneath his polished shoes and went on:

—In any case, I was passing by on the way to the office and it occurred to me it is nearly lunchtime, and I wondered . . . well, I thought, perhaps, if you're not otherwise engaged, you might consider joining me.

—Joining you?

He peeked up to gauge your reaction and dropped his head again and continued to address the planks:

—I thought, perhaps, if you're not otherwise . . . because, if you are, you see, I more than understand, and yet we both must eat . . . that is, there's a restaurant in the square with rather a nice view of the clock, and I . . . well . . . perhaps another time, perhaps another . . .

With that he turned, stepped out the door, and was swept up by pedestrians flowing past in the street.

You didn't see him again for two weeks. He walked through the door at the same time of day as before and studying the wooden planks spoke as if completing a sentence he had begun half a heartbeat ago:

—And so I thought, perhaps, you see . . . if you're not otherwise engaged, that is, you might find it in yourself to accompany me for lunch to a restaurant I frequent in the square. It has, as I say, rather a nice view. I have an appointment elsewhere at half two, but I . . .

—I'd love to, you said before he escaped again.

Mr. Samsa's head lifted. He seemed genuinely taken aback.

—Let me just put the lunch sign in the window and lock up, you said.

Outside it was a warm blue day. Mr. Samsa strolled along wordlessly beside you. The restaurant had ironwork chairs and tables and red-and-white umbrellas. The two of you exchanged a handful of phrases over the menu, but when your food arrived the conversation ceased.

You attempted to revive it, but Mr. Samsa lifted his hand and pointed to the town hall clock across the wide ocean of flat gray cobblestones and said:

—Ah, look. It's beginning.

On the day the clockmaker perfected its construction in 1490, the city council visited him in his apartments and blinded him so he wouldn't build a more beautiful clock elsewhere. Watching the hour turn, you can understand why. At a quarter till an elaborately carved door swings open, and a grand apparatus rolls out onto a wide platform. It looks like a complicated loom consisting of three parts: the Bed, the Designer, and the Harrow. In the Bed rests a human-sized puppet resembling the original clockmaker. It is strapped face down, a piece of cloth in its mouth. At ten till a skeleton with an hourglass in its right hand appears from a second door. It approaches the apparatus and pulls on a rope with its free hand. The Harrow descends and commences carving in an unreadable language what scholars believe to be a list of those things the clockmaker most missed seeing into the skin of his back.

On the hour a blade descends and decapitates him. A large wooden crow flings into an open window in the clock face and caws out the time. The Bed rises to display the bloody writing on the headless clockmaker's back before the body drops down a chute hidden in the flooring. The apparatus rolls back through the door, which closes behind.

Several people across the square clapped when the show was over, Mr. Samsa among them. Next he was rising to leave. Hand outstretched for a shake, he bowed.

—It's been a great pleasure.

—You're going? I asked.

—The appointment, you see. Business. Please call me Ulrich. I hope we will see each other again.

You once asked your mother why God took away nice people's sight if He was goodness and light. Your mother looked at you, hands on her hips. She told you to stop believing in Him immediately.

—Some things happen, she said, and some things don't. Now go live your life.

That is a little like how Ulrich courted you. When you expected him, he wouldn't show up, and when you tried to put him out of your mind, he would. Sometimes he took you to lunch. You sat in the same ironwork chairs at the same restaurant and ate the same food you had on your first date and watched the same show in silence. Sometimes you strolled along the banks of the river. He never talked about himself yet never ceased to be interested in you.

He asked what you ate for breakfast and what sort of pillow you preferred and where you would be right now if you could be anywhere else in the world except here. If you told him you didn't know, he became even more interested. How could someone not know where she wanted to be right now if she could be anywhere except here?

Sometimes you stood side by side on the bridge and watched

the dark green water rushing below. You waited for him to kiss you, but he never did. He didn't even try to hold your hand. He courted you too slowly and one day stopped coming altogether. That was almost two months ago. You waited for him and then you waited for him less and then today, this minute, you raise your chin while counting out change for Mrs. Klinghoffer and wonder whatever happened to him.

When she leaves, you take a seat on your stool behind the counter and close your eyes, deciding: *Stories with happy endings are the ones that aren't over yet.*

Seconds later the tiny bells on the door jingle crazily.

Another customer enters, a short, thick-waisted, heavy-hipped woman, her face scrunched up with determination, and, forgetting what it was you have just been thinking, you rise to meet her with a respectful smile.

margaret

The ache in Margaret's right shoulder nags her as she wanders among statuary in the Egyptian gallery. She massages it absentmindedly, then less absentmindedly. All the ligaments ache. Her muscles feel gristly. Wandering, massaging, she tries to recall if she might have banged into something recently—a doorjamb, a bedpost—but comes up blank. It felt fine as she crawled under her duvet last night.

Pausing before a behemoth stone scarab on a low pedestal, she switches her backpack from her bad to her good shoulder and straightens her black cateye glasses that don't need straightening. Thousands of dust particles revolve high in bluegray sunshine. The instant seems concentrated, singular, everything in the hall sparkly with opportunity.

The plaque beneath the scarab says it dates from the fourth century BC. A meter and a half long, it is one of the largest representations of the insect known. The scarab-god Khepera, whose name derives from the Egyptian word for *to become,* was believed to push the sun across the sky from dawn to dusk every day the same way the beetle pushed its ball of dung across the sand, and thus the beetle became associated with notions of renewal and regeneration.

Ouch, Margaret thinks, reading.

Ouch.

Switching shoulders doesn't help. She knows she should probably take two Anadin, only she doesn't like the taste and they make her chest burn. Neddie used to chew one every morning with his tea like a sugar cube. He said it was for his heart. Once, helping Nellie clear the breakfast table, little Margaret nicked one from the sap-green bottle Neddie kept on the lace runner. Thinking it was going to taste like sweet vanilla, she tried to chew it the way her grandfather did. She shudders at the recollection of the bitter white crumbs dissolving on the back of her tongue.

It strikes her, standing there, recalling, that she is quite likely inhaling atoms that were pharaohs. Pharaohs and Plato and Geoffrey Chaucer's cat.

She shudders again and moves off in the direction of the lavatory. Margaret is positive it is situated at the end of the west wing and down the stairs. She has used it a thousand times. When she enters the stairwell, though, she finds the stairs ascend rather than descend. At the top is nothing save another hall of exhibits, this time enclosed in large glass display cases. Irritated, she retraces her steps. Rather than coming out on the main floor, as she assumed she would, she finds herself on the lowest level among chunks of Greek and Roman architecture.

A Pakistani guard tilts back in his chair against the wall, feet curled around its legs, arms crossed over his potbelly like a pregnant woman. He and Margaret are the only people down here. His eyes are shut. She can't figure out whether he's really sleeping or just relaxing. Moving closer, self-conscious, she coughs into her palm to get his attention. The guard's eyes pop open. His pinkyellow tear ducts are swollen and oozy.

He doesn't uncross his arms or untilt his chair, just stares directly ahead, clearly displeased at being interrupted, while Margaret asks directions. He sends her back up to the main floor and over to the east stairs leading down to the entrance.

There she comes upon the same security line she went through twenty minutes ago. The same corpulent guard is still at it. He happens to look up the very second Margaret drifts into the open. A small recognition opens up his features.

Margaret ducks into what she presumes to be the corridor from which she exited, which turns out to be another one altogether that conducts her straight to the loo. Joggled, she slips into a vacant stall, locks the door behind her, drops her jeans, makes herself comfortable, and pees vehemently with her forehead almost touching her knees. She waits until the present wave of patrons washes away before sneaking out to the mirror.

Tugging down the right shoulder of her baggy black sweater, she has a look, and her heart becomes bees' wings. Extending from the base of her neck to her upper arm is a large purplish-green bruise.

How terribly odd, she thinks.

She digs around in her backpack and comes up with a transparent plastic container of blue breath mints, a tube of coconut-scented hand lotion from the Body Shop, a stick of vanilla lip balm, a number two pencil, the dark green lozenge of Kafka's book, a container of floss, an ivory-colored wide-toothed plastic comb, a black boar-bristle brush, a pair of miniature silver keys, her black nylon Velcro wallet, a roll of scotch tape, a packet of tissues, a pair of black wool mittens, a package of spearmint gum, and, at length, at the very bottom, her box of painkillers.

She pops two into her mouth and swallows, following them with a few palmfuls of tap water that tastes like licking a brass doorknob.

Running the brush through her hair, she dredges up a scene

of Neddie and her walking through the moors one morning when she was seven or eight.

It was early autumn. The sky was the cold whiteblue of gin on ice. Neddie's words puffed out his nose and mouth in thin white clouds that reminded Margaret of American Indians sending up smoke signals.

Did you know if you stomp your feet near a sleeping rabbit, Neddie said as they strolled, Margaret's tiny soft hand in his great coarse one, you can literally scare it to death?

They're that timid, sweet pea.

They're that high-strung.

Watch.

papa

Seeing no alternative, The Father shaves, trims his mustache, slaps on too much prickly cologne, kisses air in the general vicinity of his wife's cheek, and closes the door to his flat behind him.

He has made appointments at four banks in the neighborhood and shows up early to each, wearing his old uniform with the gold buttons Mutti has polished so thoroughly they shine like fish scales in the sun.

At the last, a junior clerk with a protruding upper lip offers him a job as messenger. The Father's duties, the junior clerk explains in a tone suggesting he considers The Father either dull, lazy, or both, will consist of fetching breakfast and lunch for the other junior clerks. The Father bows courteously, thanking him.

Inside, he seethes.

A tree is known by its fruit, and The Father is ashamed of what a weak crop his loins have engendered.

He recalls with brief affection the Christmas Georg bought them their first radio. From her nest among foil wrapping paper and unlidded boxes beneath the spruce, Mutti pointed out sweetly it was the wrong brand. It wasn't, to be perfectly honest, the one she had asked for. She had wanted a Blaupunkt, not a Brandt.

Georg apologized and replaced it the very next day. That's what a son did. Such was the natural order of things.

But Gregor?

Gregor had done exactly nothing of late except take up too much space. And what, precisely, did he give back?

The Father was at a loss to say, and so he heard himself proposing one evening after dinner, the butterypeppery waft of potato soup still plentiful in the living room air, that perhaps they could see their way clear to charge a modest sum from their neighbors and other interested parties to visit Gregor a few minutes every third day to, as it were, see the show— colorless, admittedly, as that show might be.

—Just a thought, he said, leaning back in his chair. A quick look. Nothing more. Perhaps they could even observe him at feeding time. It might prove instructive to some. The children down the block. Our way of giving something back to the community. And if that works, who knows?

Mutti objected, arguing it wasn't fair that strangers should be permitted to see Gregor and she not be permitted to join them. It is a mother's responsibility to comfort her son when he isn't feeling up to scratch, she said, yet neither Grete nor The Father had allowed her to step beyond the threshold of Gregor's door since what she had come to think of as The Accident.

That was nothing if not for her own good, they assured her, but she continued to express her misgivings.

—It is all theater with that boy, The Father said, cutting her off affectionately. We've had a hard enough time of it as it is. Do you really need further tribulations? No. I'm putting my foot down. But perhaps if the neighbors . . .

The Father regards himself as an Abraham with an Isaac not quite worth the sacrifice. His own father had been able to lift a sack of corn with his teeth. That's the kind of man he was. His mother, a woman shaped like a barrel of molasses, had given birth to and raised six children in their one-room shack in a remote village. Second-oldest, The Father was put to work as soon as he was capable of pulling a cart. In summer and winter, in bad weather and good, he made his rounds delivering slabs of meat to his father's far-flung clientele. The foot sores he suffered! There were afternoons when every step came to him as a shock of lightning. But did he ever contemplate abandoning his work?

The month he turned fourteen, his mother gave him a warm-hearted hug, his father a few small bills, and with that he was sent off to the city to make his own way in the world. Despite the competition from the other peddlers, despite his feeling continuously cut loose in a squall, The Father survived. He even prospered, in a manner of speaking, and he shared that prosperity with his parents in monthly letters home.

On his seventeenth birthday he enlisted in the military because that is what a decent, fit young man did when his country needed him.

All that hardship, all that struggle—and yet somehow in the end The Father had managed to turn out perfectly well. But his son? His son, who never lacked a thing, has taken to sitting naked in the dark, staring out his window, brooding about heaven knows what.

God, The Father is quite sure, is testing his family in order to make it stronger. The Father very much doubts his family is up to the challenge.

It is time, he decides, to put such disagreeable matters behind him. It is time to get on with it. Besides, everyone knows the devil dances in an empty pocket. And so, just as in the olden days, every morning The Father rises with the light. Before striking off, he eats a hearty breakfast, performs his ablutions, dresses, and consults his tidy reflection in the looking glass in the foyer.

He very much likes what he sees there. What he sees is a man who has done what he has to do, refuses to shirk his responsibilities. No one can doubt The Father works quite hard for a fellow his age. He takes his new job seriously. He returns home each day by mid-afternoon, in plenty of time for a well-earned beer before dinner, and, although it isn't the sort of post that provides an abundance of riches, exactly, it is the sort that allows The Father to stay on top of most of the family's debts, so long as Mutti and Grete chip in, so long as he keeps a close eye on the accounts.

If he were to be completely frank, The Father would have to confess that his uniform fills him with a certain degree of verve. He can feel the thing peeling off the years, carrying him back to better days, and for that reason he makes the decision almost without thought never to take it off except when asleep or bathing. He wears it at work, but also at the table for the evening meal, and afterward, as he settles back into his easy chair and begins to doze, washcloth on his heart, listening contentedly to the voices of his wife and daughter admonishing each other to be quieter.

Although his eyelids are lowered, The Father can picture Mutti bending low over her lamp, stitching away at pieces of underwear for that new firm that hired her just last week, while Grete teaches herself shorthand and French on the couch with a view to bettering herself and moving on from the position she took last month as a salesgirl into something more promising.

Sometimes The Father wakes with a start without being

completely aware that he has ever coasted away from wakeful-
ness and announces for no particular reason:

—What a lot of sewing you're doing today!

Then he whiffs away again.

The family can only afford dry-cleaning and pressing inter-
mittently, often no more than once every month or six weeks.
Not brand-new to start with, The Father's uniform soon shows
a faint fraying around the neck and cuffs, crumples around the
sleeves and seat, stains and shreds of sauerkraut and bread-
crumbs down the front like an accretion of tiny barnacles on
the dark blue hull of a sunken ship.

After work, he refuses to contemplate changing back into
his robe. He dozes late into the night, until he becomes aware
of his wife plucking gently at his sleeve. Far off, he hears his
daughter setting down her books and rising to help. The Father feels them hoisting him up by the armpits, guiding him
ponderously down the hall, past his useless son's room, toward
the gorgeous pliability of his own bed, and, more often than he
cares to admit, he hears his own voice muttering from some
fatigued distance as he makes his way toward a kind of tem-
porary reprieve:

—So this is a life. The peace and quiet of my old age. Who
would have thought it? Who?

grete

The night before my third date with Herrmann, I have a dream.

I open the door to feed my zombie brother one morning and find him changed into an enormous plant made out of skin instead of cellulose. His body has swallowed up the chair by the window and seeped out across the room, growing over the desk, the couch, the bed, one wall, even taking part of the rug into it. A single eye high in the corner blinks down at me. Gregor is everywhere.

—Beyond a certain point there is no return, his mouth says where the photograph of that model used to hang. This is the point that must be reached. Guess what color I'm thinking of.

—Oh, Gregor, I say, sighing, setting down his food tray on a piece of him that contains a lattice of fleshy veins, a mosaic of toenail chips. Papa won't be very happy, you know.

—Little can be learned without opening me up. Then you will see there are two kinds of milk: the kind you drink when you're awake, and the kind you drink when you're sleeping. If you thought *mauve*, I'm sorry to say you are wrong.

—Don't talk in riddles.

—It's your dream, not mine. No . . . wait. It's my dream, not yours. Have you seen my kneecaps?

I pretend I am not listening. Sitting back on my heels, I

remove a knife and fork I didn't know I was carrying in my apron. I lean forward, slice off a small shaving of him, place it on my tongue.

It melts like a delicious chocolate leaf.

Outside, flurries frantic the cold gray Sunday. The odor of smoldering rats sharpens the air, but less than before. Herrmann is late. Gregor was always scrupulous about everything else in his life, but the time he kept wasn't our time. He always looked stunned and apologized profusely when someone pointed out that he was expected somewhere forty minutes earlier. The next day he would stand them up again as if the day before had never happened.

I wait ten minutes, fifteen, beneath the stone arch of the gothic tower, blowing into my cupped hands, thinking about my dream, observing hordes of passersby pouring along. Everyone is dressed in black. Black coats, black boots, black hats. They remind me of a murder of hunched crows peg-legging through the snow on their way back from church.

Just as I'm beginning to worry, Herrmann swings around the corner with a bright smile and wave. Then I see the large bruise around his right eye, down his right cheek. Straightaway I feel dreadful for being annoyed.

—Oh, nothing, really, he says when I ask. Bit of a disagreement with some of the White Resistance boys.

—You look awful!

—I made a few suggestions as I passed a—what do you call it?—a *pod* of them in the street. Apparently they had other ideas about how to spend their day than those I offered. He laughs and gives me a quick hug. It's wonderful to see you again, he says. High point of the whole bloody week.

We strike off at a leisurely pace, cross the bridge lined with dark statues of martyrs and prophets, and cut up into the maze of progressively narrower and more winding lanes near the castle.

On every third or fourth corner stands a young soldier in a worn olive uniform selling off his war medals for extra cash. Short old women swathed in thick shawls hawk bratwursts from steaming carts. Then the crowds thin out, fall away, and soon we are all by ourselves, strolling down a cobbled alley with one- and two-story whitewashed buildings on either side, doors and shuttered windows glossy black. Herrmann has his arm around my waist. We talk about nothing special, my boring new job at the sweets shop, the way the lightly falling snow makes everything appear slow and ghostly like you are visiting a memory of a memory.

I listen to the rhythm of our heels clicking below us, the distant clock cawing the hour, the tenor of his bassoon voice. Shutting my eyes, I slant into the presence of his arm, the pinprick flakes of cold tapping my face and vanishing, and begin to imagine myself suspended in the center of a gigantic piece of marzipan. It is white and soft and grainy with almond paste and sugar. Behind the immediate scents lingers an understated vanilla that makes me forget all the French verbs I have been trying to learn.

Then I become conscious of a heavy pressure against my tummy and chest, and I open my eyes again.

It is Herrmann.

My back is against one of the whitewashed walls. He is leaning into me, muttering something I can't make out, kissing my throat.

I try to raise my palms to ease him away, remind him how a

gentleman behaves, but he holds my wrists, pinning my arms down by my sides.

—Herrmann, I say.

He doesn't pay any attention.

—Herrmann.

He is listening to nothing but his own voice now.

The one slipping out of tune.

The one burning my neck.

the neighbor

To forget about writing, the author who lives alone in the flat directly below the Samsas sometimes visualizes himself as a piece of furniture. A footstool. A side table. Nothing expensive, nothing elaborate. It gets his mind off his fiction and back to being a petty clerk for the workmen's insurance company. Arriving home late every afternoon, he takes a short nap, eats a small plain dinner, opens his notebook, and gets down to what really matters to him. He writes through the night and into the early morning hours, breaking off only when his insomniac brain refuses to spin any longer, then steals a few hours' sleep and rises at five o'clock to wash and dress for the office. Twenty-nine years old, he has yet to publish anything except one short story about the reconciliation between a domineering father and his wayward son, of which he is less than proud. Whenever he picks up his pencil, he feels time running out around him. Next summer he will turn thirty and have nothing to show for it save a mediocre situation in a cubicle that smells of correction fluid, mildew, and gloom. Presently he is lying on his back in his neatly made bed, staring up at the ceiling, hands fisted upon his belly, picturing a fully clothed version of himself composing at the desk in front of the window overlooking the dreary gray hospital across the dreary gray street almost wholly swallowed by fog. This secondary version will manage everything efficiently while the primary one rests a minute or two. He has been working since seven on what he believes will be a novella called *Pleasure: Theories of Forgetting.* It is based on the odd noises emanating from the flat above him. Clumps. Scratching sounds. An almost continuous mumbling whose words the author cannot discern, no matter how diligently he concentrates. *What sort of universe is happening up there?* he asked himself over dinner. That is when the idea for the novella coasted into sight. The story will be a kind of . . . what's the word? The story will be a kind of fairy tale. No, parable. No, allegory. In it, a man will awake with meat cleavers for hands. The moral will be that the meaning of life is that it stops. The ending will be happy, although the author is still unsure how he will get from here to there.

No, he decides, lying there, hands fisted, pondering what he has written so far this evening.

No.

That won't do at all.

He rises, crosses to his desk, and draws a large X through each page of his notebook.

He begins again.

grete

Maybe this is what you are supposed to do. Maybe his breath is supposed to smell like that and maybe this is the kind of thing he is supposed to say. Maybe it is supposed to feel like this now but feel different later. Maybe that is why no one tells you about what it will feel like beforehand. Maybe you are supposed to think about something else and then he will stop and then you can go to the café and have a nice cup of hot cocoa and pretend it didn't happen. Maybe you can just stand here doing nothing except thinking of something else and then later you will call it something else and remember it as something else and then you will start to feel better because this is what they mean when they say that word. This is what they mean when they say it because

the chambermaid

he only intended to stay that night do some business then train home next day for Christmas celebrate with family but the snow started falling in the afternoon scatter of flurries then more then a whiteout so you couldn't see the garden from the lobby all the trains canceled him stranded here only guest in the hotel and everyone feeling sorry for him eating breakfast by himself in the corner of the dining room and him so handsome in a quiet way keeping to himself till I knocked on his door just past ten asked if I might make up his room and *how old are you?* he asked standing there the door ajar him in his bathrobe those his exact words *how old are you?* and I said *beg pardon* and he said *how old?* and I said *sixteen sir* because that was almost true and he said *you should be home with your mother and father over the holidays* and I said *they live in the country sir I'm high and dry as you are sir* and that's how we started chatting each other up me tidying the room changing towels him asking me all manner of questions me dizzy because no one ever asked so many and him having more important things to do but there we were in the end sitting side by side on his bed him in just his robe simply talking mind you but it was his mouth I don't know why I wanted to reach out touch it with my fingertips him being so considerate the thought of it but that's what I wanted if he had at that minute moved closer my hand would have been at his lips showing him what I learned last summer on that sickly hot afternoon up at the mill lying in the grass stream flowing above our heads getting all sloppy down there falling into his eyes saying with mine *here I am help yourself sir* only he didn't no but stopped talking looked at me said *put on your coat and mittens let me show you something* and before I knew it we had flung ourselves into the snowstorm you could see something loosening in his face him saying without saying how he didn't much care for my body but don't feel bad because he didn't much care for his own neither no didn't much care for no one's all those innards sloshing around because all he wanted was to play the way everything looked like it was somewhere else because of the whiteness thick in the air so without a thought he bent scooped up a handful of snow threw it at me hitting me square in the shoulder me laughing doing the same only girlarm swerving far left and off we went chasing each other through the garden throwing snowballs because no one seemed to mind because it was Christmas with nothing else to do nowhere else to be our clothes heavywet hair knotted cheeks redpink and *I'm so glad you were here* he told me before we went in to change walking through the front door reappearing an hour later dressed in a fine suit in the dining room where he ate alone smiling at me civilly me moving back and forth helping the cook as if we had never met and while I was in the kitchen he took his leave I couldn't do nothing except wait till knocking on his door next morning ask if he'd like his room tidied but when I did it was nine o'clock and there was no answer because he had left at dawn the manager telling me he took the first train out to hurry home to his wife children because they'd be worried and *what there isn't is what we haven't wished for hard enough* I thought because we were ourselves again the day itself again so I shrugged because the manager was looking at me I had plenty of work to do so I went back

margaret

What Margaret likes most about reading in special places is how it makes her feel nothing exists except herself and the planet on the page.

Sneakers off, feet tucked up under her at one of the long tables beneath the gold-leafed dome, she is lost. She loves how Kafka doesn't use a showy style or look-at-me gimmicks. How she can picture all the details so clearly—Uwe's thin little legs wriggling helplessly before his eyes, the swath of small white spots spread across his belly. Where in the world did Kafka come up with such ideas? Margaret wishes she had that kind of imagination.

Uwe is an insect on the outside but a human being on the inside, just like everyone else. Yet he is no more surprised by his new situation than if he had awakened with a sore throat. His existence has altered thunderously with the very first sentence of the story, only all he wants to do is get up and get to work on time so people won't yell at him. What happened to him has simply happened. Kafka doesn't explain Uwe's condition. He doesn't spell things out. Every so often some people turn into bugs while others don't. The change is quick, irresistible. The notion gives Margaret the creeps.

And why, she asks herself, twirling a short strand of black hair between thumb and index finger, idly taking in her surroundings, are there so many doors in the Samsa flat? Why are so many of them locked, all the rooms stuffy?

And speaking of rooms, she is having a serious problem determining how many there are and they are all supposed to fit together. Uwe's seems to be located between his sister's and the living room, connected to each and to a hallway by separate doors, which is rather an odd configuration for a flat, if you stop to think about it. Margaret imagines Uwe the center of a constricted solar system. His room is described thoroughly, but the farther from it you go, the fuzzier the rest of the solar system becomes.

Where exactly, for instance, is his parents' room? Where do the cook and servant girl sleep? And what, besides that bleak hospital, exists beyond the fog outside the window?

At any rate, Margaret is sure she doesn't much care for the characters. Uwe's father is an insensitive bully, chelping at everyone just for the fun of it. There his son is, transformed into a bug (Margaret has a vague suspicion Uwe keeps changing size and variety as the story progresses), and all the guy can do is complain and thump on his son's door.

The mother, whiny handwringer that she is, isn't much better, although Margaret does hold out a dash of hope for the sister. At least she seems genuinely concerned about what's happening to her brother.

And then there's the mean chief clerk. Why would someone like that travel all the way from his office to Uwe's flat for no other purpose than to badger and threaten his employee minutes after he fails to show up for work on time?

What a terribly squirrelly bunch.

The more Margaret mulls it all over, the more peculiar it becomes. Perhaps she will find out what it's all about at the book club this evening. If nothing else, it will be interesting to hear what everyone else has to say, so long as there aren't a lot of people smarter than she is there. Margaret positively loathed sitting in classes at the poly listening to prats who loved to hear themselves drone on and on.

What if she shows up only to find the others already have the book sorted out? What if *The Metamorphosis* is supposed to be easy and Margaret has missed the whole point because she doesn't know how to read very well because she never applied herself in school?

Margaret wonders how many books she has read over the course of her lifetime, and she worries the number is not nearly as high as she might have hoped. She watches herself raising her hand at the World's End to add what she believes to be a not unintelligent remark, only to discover everyone turning to scrutinize her in the way bored aunts and uncles turn to scrutinize nephews who stand at attention at crowded holiday dinner tables to announce with great pomp that they are possessed of x-ray vision.

Margaret wishes she had paid more attention to her lit professor. She tries to recall his name, realizes she probably never knew it in the first place.

Letting go the strand of hair, she reaches down, turns the page, pushes on.

the servant girl

Grete is wearing two love bites on her neck. Dark purple stains below her left ear. I see them as I stoop to refill her water glass at the dinner table. They weren't there this morning, before she went on another date with that lieutenant. She tells me what a gentleman he is, but gentlemen don't leave that sort of thing on a girl's neck. It looks like something with pincers went after her.

I cross to where the missus is sitting to refill her glass, and she starts in again. She wants to see her son. She wants to see him tonight. For weeks she hasn't brought up the subject. I thought she had forgotten.

A month after The Accident, she took to walking up and down the staircase to the street. Up, down. Up, down. She wouldn't change out of her robe. Soon as the master left for the day, she commenced. She did it until Grete came home early one afternoon and caught her.

The master of the house is in the middle of describing how today he delivered lunch to a very important junior clerk. If you get too close to him, you can smell his uniform. Like bedding you sleep in all winter.

—I have a *right* to see him, the missus barges in. Can't either of you understand? I have a *right*.

She bangs down her spoon on the table. Her lentil soup glops over the side of her bowl. I turn the muscles in my face into sleeping cats.

—But Mutti, says Grete softly. We've had this conversation before.

—Pardon me, says the master less softly. I was trying to tell a story. It isn't everyone who finds himself allowed to . . .

—You and your stupid stories, the missus says to the ceiling.

The master of the house leans back slowly, like a shot bear, staring at her.

—Excuse me?

The missus examines a hairline crack jagging through the plaster above her.

—My son is sick, she explains to it. I want to see him. I won't take no for an answer.

A hush pushes across the room.

Then the master sneezes a sneeze into his cupped palms that contains all the rage of the cosmos within it.

The missus jumps in her seat.

Silverware and china jangle.

—Gesundheit, says Grete.

—Thank you, the master says, sniffling daintily.

While he and Grete exchange courtesies, the missus pushes her chair back and makes a trundling rush toward Gregor's door.

I step aside. I lower my head. I don't want to be part of this. Grete balls up her napkin and prepares to follow, but the master is already there, holding the missus back, arms snug around her. He whispers things into her ear to soothe her.

—Stop it this instant, he coos. I forbid it. I won't have this kind of behavior in my house.

The missus is crying.

Crying and gasping.

She is pointing with a limp arm toward her son's locked door.

—This isn't right, she sobs. Both of you. Keeping a mother

from her boy like this. You should be ashamed of yourselves. *Ashamed.*

The next afternoon Grete returns early from work and informs the missus she has a plan. I am cooking in the kitchen. I can hear her talking in the living room but can't make out the specific words, so I step over to the door and press my ear against it.

—Gregor doesn't need all that furniture in there, Grete is saying. It just takes up room. He doesn't even use most of it. I'm thinking perhaps we could make a little extra something selling off a few pieces. The chest of drawers. The writing desk. It would help with our payments. Lend me a hand? We could have them on the landing and fetch the furniture salesman round by the time Papa gets home.

I unlock the kitchen door and steal up the hallway. My excuse will be to ask them if they might fancy a cup of tea. The missus is already heading toward Gregor's door when I arrive. Her exclamations die away as she approaches. I see her hands turning fidgety before her. The fingers of the left begin bothering the fingers of the right.

Grete sees what is happening, too. She steps around her mother and enters first to make sure the coast is clear. She reappears and, smiling affectionately, takes the missus by the wrist. I can hear them beginning to wrestle with something very large and heavy in there. It takes quite a long time. At length, I hear the missus say they might as well leave the chest of drawers where it is. It weighs too much. She is already out of breath.

—Besides, she says, wheezing, maybe it's not such a good idea to take away Gregor's things. I mean, won't it look to him as if we've given up?

—Nonsense. This thing means nearly one month's rent for us. Imagine how pleased Papa will be. It's as if Gregor is still helping us, isn't it?

—I just think it might be a nice gesture . . .

—It would be a *lovely* gesture, Mutti. But we've got commitments. Bills to pay. Let's see if we can't just . . .

Stillness follows. You can hear the missus considering. I stand near the entrance to the living room, biding my time. It occurs to me how rare and pleasing instants like this are, when you don't have anyone else to listen to.

Slowly the chest of drawers emerges through the door. Grete is pushing. Behind her, the missus supervises. She looks pasty and uncomfortable. Grete halts, examining the fruits of her labor. She goes back into Gregor's room to tackle the writing desk.

The missus hangs behind in the living room, consulting the window, the photographs framed behind the dining table. Either she doesn't notice me standing there or doesn't care when she does. She turns and steps back into Gregor's room to join her daughter.

Immediately her screams begin flying out.

Reaching the doorway, I see her collapsed backward across the sofa. Her arms are outspread like she is about to receive someone on top of her, her eyes rolled up in her head. You can see the whites but not the colored parts.

Across from her, Gregor presses his belly and chest against the wall, trying to cover something up. His face is turned so I can tell his eyes are also shut. His skin is unhealthy, his shaggy hair and beard tangled. He is in a state of nature. My throat makes a sound for me: a backward hiccup.

Grete hurries past, barking something about smelling salts. In a single graceful motion, Gregor spins around to see where she has gone and bounds after her. I want to move, only it is like standing on the shore watching a ship sinking on the horizon. You have to see what happens next, even though you feel you already know.

In the living room, a bottle breaks.

—*Gregor!* Grete shouts.

He is running, knocking into things. A side table cracks against the floorboards. A lamp crashes. Someone kicks the door shut behind me. The bang jolts the missus awake. Her eyes spring open. They dart around her in panic. She doesn't look like she knows where she is or what brought her here.

I think to myself, *at least things can't get any worse.* There is some comfort in that. Then the master of the house storms through the front door, bellowing:

—*What in God's name is going on here?*

His voice sounds like Yahweh talking to Noah.

—*Mutti's fainted!* Grete shouts. *Gregor's loose!*

—*Just as I expected!* he roars, thundering up the hallway. *Just as I expected! What have I been telling you? But you women! You never listen! Step aside, step aside! Let me take care of this . . .*

The Lord is trying to make them all better through their misfortune, but I don't think they are paying very much attention.

mutti

For my birthday — I remember — princess trapped in the sofa tower — prince crawling up the chair ladder to save her — precious Georg our ogre with the umbrella club — but it all just — I don't know — when my shortbread boy returned — the vanilla scent had left him — you could hear him in his bedroom — awake for days on end — when he reappeared — our world wasn't what he was expecting to find — he told me — he poked his head out his door and told me — he no longer cared for the color orange — what an idea — always forgetting things — always behind schedule — but over the course of months — things eased back to normal — more or less — give or take — simple enough to overlook the smallest slips — the shut mouth catches no flies — and when Papa fell on hard times Gregor was there — everything for a purpose — that's how it — but my shortbread boy — hugging him was hugging a golem — the way he stood there — biding his time till I let go — eyes doll eyes — arms doll arms — they say mothers don't have favorites — but they can't help it — precious Georg gone — and now him — every growing up a growing away — you try to convince yourself otherwise — you think to yourself — *this too will pass* — my son took my son away — *what a beautiful boy!* they used to say — *look at that hair!* — you think to yourself — *don't make a fuss* — *he'll come back* — *be patient* — *that's all you have to* — but the months pass — you try to keep up your spirits — the months pass — and then one day you realize a stranger is living in his room — the look he gave — charging me — nowhere to be seen then there he was — rushing from behind the couch — my feet going out from under me — and what — who's over — the uproar — it's as if — as if my heart's gone — yes — good — that's good — then there will be nothing left to break —

ραρα

Ah, good shot! thinks The Father, pegging another apple at Gregor cowering outside his door. *You see. I've still got it in me. I've still got the stuff it takes. Let them say what they will, but I've still got that.*

The Father is surprised by his own vigor, by how over the last several weeks he has felt the fresh warm tide of it flowing back into his veins. He is no longer that old fellow who used to go out with his family one or two Sundays a year plus the high holy days, shuffling between his wife and Gregor with the help of his crook-handled stick. No longer that old fellow who of necessity had to come to a full standstill on the street and gather his escort around him whenever he had something to say.

All that weariness has fallen away, the heavy fatigue that made it seem he was dragging a sack full of sand from each ankle. In that old fellow's place rises a new man in a smart blue uniform. Straight-spined, The Father envisions how his dark brown eyes must be flashing beneath his bushy white eyebrows as he closes the distance between himself and his son, how his white mustache must be a-twitch with power. He envisions the imposing figure he must be cutting in the middle of this living room in the middle of this crisp wintry afternoon, and he wouldn't have it any other way.

When he inhales it feels as if he is inhaling pride itself. He is here. He is back. He is at the top of his game. When everything is said and done, The Father believes, plowing forward, a man must do what a man must do to defend his family, and The Father is doing it: he is bombarding his son with apples.

He boomed through the doorway to discover Gregor in the midst of a juvenile display, scuttling around every which way, upsetting furniture, ramming walls, grunting and menacing his sister with his sweaty face, and The Father took action without delay. Grim-visaged, tails of his jacket flapping up behind him, he strode right at him, picking up two fistfuls of apples from the dish on the sideboard as he passed. He stuffed a few in each pocket and launched the first volley as he stepped around the toppled side table, over the smashed lamp.

The Father threw with precision and gusto. It felt wonderful. The preliminary projectile clonked the wall next to his son's head. Gregor came to an abrupt stop in alarm. He looked around frantically, then commenced zigzagging in an effort to evade the looming attack. He halted when The Father halted, scurried forward when The Father made any move. In this way, the two of them circled the room twice without anything decisive happening.

Yet the truth was Gregor's military training and experience were no match for The Father's. In quick succession, before Gregor even had time to contemplate a response, let alone act upon it, The Father lobbed a second apple and a third.

The latter caught the layabout behind the left knee. He hopped straight up in astonishment and landed in a stagger.

That got his attention, all right. There was, the boy could plainly see, no further reason to continue running. There was nowhere to run to. He turned and pawed rapidly at the plaster, trying to scurry up it toward the ceiling. The Father zeroed in. He fired off a fourth, fifth, and sixth volley. With each shot, he sensed his aim improving.

And now, flushed with the whiff of victory, he lets loose the seventh and eighth. Both graze off Gregor's shoulder and send him huddling before his closed door.

The ninth nails him squarely in the jaw.

Gregor yips and shields his head with his arms.

The door behind him blasts open.

The Father's wife, wearing nothing but her underbodice, tears forward. The servant girl, The Father infers, raising his last apple, testing its smooth globular solidity in his palm, must have loosened Mutti's clothing to let her breathe more freely in the wake of her swoon. She dodges around her cringing son and past her flummoxed daughter (run-down automaton, Grete ceased moving the second the shelling commenced), through the chaos of apples rolling about on the floor, and, unswervingly, at The Father himself.

Mutti throws herself around his neck, whimpering, struggling for breath, begging and begging for her son's life.

grete

I know where I shall find him this morning. I shall find him beneath the sofa, discolored sheet tugged down over him, bare foot sticking out at the far end, toes curled, eyes squeezed shut to keep me out.

But he can't keep me out.

I am here, squatting, pinching up the curtain of the miniature stage, come to scold him:

—The scare you gave Mutti. It was dreadful. *Dreadful.* Do you know where she's been ever since? In bed. *In bed,* Gregor. And it's all because of you.

Outside it is trying to be dawn but having trouble because the first snow of the year is sifting down in a thick grainy mist like salt. It makes it seem there is no exterior to the world: everything is contained, inside something else. I watch the top of his head, wondering how you get from this place to any other. Papa planted a grape-sized plum beneath his left ear.

I think: our family is stranded in this flat.

I think: it is a raft on the wide-open ocean, only with walls.

I see myself squatting there like somebody else.

—Are you proud of yourself? Is that what you are? You broke a lamp and side table. Mutti's vial of smelling salts. And the rest of us watching every pfennig. Don't you love Papa and Mutti anymore? Don't you care about their feelings?

I wait, although I don't know what I am waiting for. Last night I couldn't sleep, occupied with what I was going to say to him, but I forgot to consider how he might or might not respond. I watch the top of his head, rubbing the things Herrmann left on my neck. They will be gone in a week. You hardly even notice them any longer unless you look carefully.

Herrmann wouldn't stop apologizing. His eyes sparkled with tears. You read about such things in books, but his actually did. Sometimes, he said, he is too romantic for his own good. His passions kick loose from him, and then he doesn't know what he is doing. Tell him how to make it up, he told me. Tell him how to behave.

I have never seen a man cry before. It made me feel smushy, sorry for us both standing there on that empty snowy street.

What else can you do except forgive him?

Herrmann said, clearing his throat, rubbing his nose, he thought he might be falling in love with me.

It takes so little to repent, no more than a pure spirit, the resolve to change. Anyone can fit the pieces of the jigsaw puzzle together. People do it every day. When at first you look, all you see are thousands of bits of color and shape. Search for the corners, then the borders, and gradually the image settles into place. You don't even reflect about it, really. Everything naturally shifts toward sense. But Gregor refuses. He won't even try. Watching, I am sure he knows what I am about to say before I say it.

—I am going to have to punish you, you know, I tell him. It doesn't please me any more than it does you. You don't appreciate what we've done for you. All you think about is yourself.

There are scabs, some the size of pinkie fingernails, across the top of his scalp where he won't stop picking.

—There will be no food today, I say. None today. None tomorrow.

At first you don't see them all through his hair.

Then you do.

—It's for your own good, I say. A lesson. You must learn it by heart.

Neither Mutti nor I say anything when Papa shows up after work with Mrs. Klinghoffer. In her sequined cucumber-green dress, pearl strings, and diamond earrings, she looks like someone on her way to a ball. Papa told us over breakfast what he was planning to do. His tone said there was no space among his ideas for an argument from us, nothing for us to do except put on our Sunday best and ask the servant girl to tidy up the living room, set the dining table, have tea waiting. Mutti requested scones with clotted cream and raspberry jam. Papa said that would be acceptable.

Mrs. Klinghoffer started inquiring about Gregor soon after The Accident. Since then, whenever she bumped into Papa on the staircase she would comment casually about how she hadn't seen him for quite a long time and how she hoped he wasn't working too hard. Papa always thanked her for her concern, saying Gregor was away on another extended business trip. He could tell at once she didn't believe him, but he kept to his story.

This morning he stopped by her flat on his way out, explained matters to her more fully, and invited her over to have a look for herself.

She agreed to pay in advance.

—What a pleasure to see you again! Mutti exclaims too cheerfully as Mrs. Klinghoffer enters the living room. Are those new earrings? How stunning!

Mrs. Klinghoffer nods vacantly, examining her surroundings

as if they were the inside of a filthy barn. Without turning, she hands her fox-fur boa over her shoulder to Papa who, waiting behind her with an attendant's thoughtfulness, receives it. He bows. We take our seats around the dining table. The servant girl pours tea. We wait for Mrs. Klinghoffer to help herself to the first scone, then we help ourselves. The afternoon tastes like a holiday.

Straight off, mouth full of biscuit pap, Mrs. Klinghoffer ignites with gossip. Did we know the petty clerk renting below us has contracted tuberculosis? She heard it from the butcher boy. They say he got it from the milk. That's how it's going around. He has a new girlfriend: an overweight socialist who collects ceramic gnomes and faeries. Can you believe it? And in his condition!

That cute cashier in the milliner's shop on the square? Dead. Crushed by a runaway cart as she left work yesterday. Stepped out of the door, locked it behind her, and walked right into it. There is some talk that she may have had Arab blood.

Something about the smeary greenish-orange makeup makes it seem Mrs. Klinghoffer is grinning as she speaks.

Papa makes a clacking noise with his tongue against the roof of his mouth to signal his indignity with the present state of things. The rest of us concur. The conversation flags, a gust of boredom passing over Mrs. Klinghoffer's features. Papa takes a sip of his Earl Grey and suggests it may be a good time to have a peek in the back room.

Mrs. Klinghoffer perks up.

I remain at the table with Mutti. She goes on nervously about nothing while staring at Gregor's door. I can hear her lungs contracting as she prattles away.

Three or four minutes, and Papa and Mrs. Klinghoffer reappear. I can see the visit didn't go well. Papa is crestfallen. Mrs. Klinghoffer is singularly unimpressed. Gregor wouldn't come out from under the sofa, she said, wouldn't utter a sound, did nothing save lie there like a rug. What sort of demonstration is *that*? And the room! The writing desk and chest of drawers cluttering the center at odd angles impeded one's view. It was like visiting an attic. The stench was . . . uncivilized.

More small talk and, despite our best efforts, Mrs. Klinghoffer departs.

Over the course of the next fortnight she sends up a small handful of neighbors, among them the family from the third floor with the two blond frog-faced children deficient in clear gender. Perhaps she does so out of compassion. Perhaps she simply can't stop herself from tittle-tattle and tall tales.

Either way, the reaction is the same. The visitors are disappointed. You can't blame them. On the street they can see the miniature bearded fat lady, drowning in her own fleshy excess, gnaw the head off a writhing puppy. Her act comes with three torches and a chorus of pink-cheeked girls singing nursery rhymes. What's so special about a man who lives under a couch?

It is the same thing that happened to hunger artistry, only more so. At least the fasters possessed a talent. My big brother possesses nothing at all.

When the frog-faced children begin to snivel, Papa digs into his pocket and gives the parents their money back. Everything Mrs. Klinghoffer told them about us shapes their faces. Papa adds a few extra pfennigs for some sweets for the little ones. Then he brings up in an offhanded manner his appeal that they consider keeping what they have seen, substandard as it is, to themselves. The less the authorities are involved in one's private lives, the better. Don't they agree?

They do, more or less.

Mutti reaches out and pats one of the youngsters on the head.

The child unhurriedly retracts its neck down into its shoulders and sticks out its chubby intestinal-red tongue without blinking.

the servant girl

A knock on the kitchen door. It is almost nine o'clock in the evening. I am cleaning up for the day.

—The master of the house, announces the master of the house when I ask who it is.

He would like to have a word with me. I unlock the door and he edges into the room like a man edging into a stranger's ideas. He is too big for the kitchen, and he knows it. You can see him trying to shrink. When that doesn't work, he talks.

—Your services will no longer be required, he says.

I don't look at him. I look at a cockroach feeling its way along the countertop, its shell a shiny licorice drop, remembering the dream I had last night. I was tidying the flat, only time was running backward. With each swirl of my dust rag, more rather than less dust appeared on the furniture. When I touched a lamp or chair, it didn't straighten, but tilted at an angle. The more I worked, the messier the flat became.

—Yes, sir, I say.

—You may collect your things and depart after breakfast to-morrow morning.

—Yes, sir.

—I regret to inform you I shall be unable to provide you with your closing wages until the end of next month. Circumstances make this unavoidable.

—Yes, sir.

—I apologize.

—Yes, sir. Is there . . . May I ask if there is something about my work you don't approve of, sir?

—Your work has been perfectly acceptable, Anna.

—There is nothing I might have changed to make it more to your liking, sir?

—I shall be happy to pen a letter to your subsequent employer, if that's what you're after.

—Yes, sir. Thank you, sir.

—Good night, Anna.

—Good night, sir.

I lock the door behind him, and everything is different. It isn't the kitchen it was five minutes ago. But it doesn't matter. I will find new employment. I will begin looking tomorrow, and I will find new employment.

Then I will buy those shoes.

Then I will start saving again. When I have enough, I will sail to America. Last month the cook's niece went. The butcher's brother left last week. In this country, everything exciting has already happened. In America, everything exciting will happen tomorrow.

I have seen pictures. You take a big ship. You cross an ocean. You step off and become whatever you want. I will become a lift operator in one of the grand hotels that grow straight up out of the wheat fields in San Francisco.

—Floor, please, I will say to the guests.

They will tell me where they want to go, and I will take them there.

The building I will work in will be so tall that from the top you have to look down to see the clouds.

It will be just like living in heaven.

margaret

Finishing the second part, the one that concludes with the apple-lobbing scene, Margaret is ready for a break.

It is tough to conceive how this story could possibly have an uplifting ending, but that's what her professor said. It just seems to get worse and worse. If you were to plot it out on a piece of paper, you would have to start at the upper left corner and draw a big heavy black line straight to the lower right, the trajectory of a little stickman skidding down the side of a glass mountain.

Margaret trawls through her backpack for her blue breath mints, pops two into her mouth, and, sucking, flips to the essays at the back of the book.

grete

If he promises to be nice, I tell him, if he promises to behave himself and not bother anyone, I shall leave his door ajar for half an hour after dinner.

It will do him good to hear the family going about its business. Papa and Mutti playing cards at the lamp-lit table as they have done almost every Sunday since they were married nearly thirty years ago. Me thumbing through my books, reciting my French lessons.

J'écoute, tu écoutes, il–elle écoute.

Nous écoutons, vous écoutez, ils–elles écoutent.

I am getting better every day. It is not an easy process, what with there being no teacher to help me, but I am getting better. Even our new addition, the enormous-boned charwoman who comes by late mornings and early evenings to do the rough work, has told me so. Her last employers came from Paris. She says I sound like them.

White-haired widow with green-flecked eyes, she reminds me of a polar bear in a too-small gray dress riding a tricycle in the traveling circus. She is riding her tricycle now, lumbering around us, dusting, rattling, panting with labor, half-humming a handful of atonal bars I cannot quite place.

We all try very hard not to notice her.

Satisfactory help isn't as easy to come by as it used to be.

I shall leave his door ajar for half an hour after dinner in the evening, I tell him, because I am feeling guilty. I have forgotten to feed him. I don't know when it started to slip my mind. Life is so full these days. It is difficult keeping track of everything you must accomplish. Lying in bed several nights ago, hovering over an inviting foggy chasm tinged with blue, a stunning opal sleep, the pin of it pricked me. I don't know how it happened. Still, I am convinced that I have never overlooked my duties for more than a day or two at a time. Surely no more than three.

Like Alice in that children's book, I must run twice as fast to stay in place. Evenings are for lessons. I see Herrmann three times a week in the afternoon. I help Mutti around the flat whenever I can. It has been a hard transition for me, leaving the sweets shop and settling into my new job in the little boutique a block off the square. I work there five mornings a week selling religious goods that have become popular since news arrived that the natural disasters had crossed the Volga.

Gold-embossed cards of encouragement. Carved and polished guardian angels for the front door. Gilt-framed poems in gothic cursive reminding us that God sees, God knows, God hears, God cares, God understands, God provides.

When I first arrived, I wondered what sort of people believed these trinkets could slow the natural disasters' progress. By the end of the first morning, I learned the answer was bricklayers, lawyers, chimney sweeps, members of the city council, flower girls, librarians, physicians, candlestick makers, young nuns, mothers, midwives, fathers, butcher boys, policemen, artists, teachers, servants, street musicians, and frightened schoolchildren.

Everyone.

Everyone in the whole city.

The shop is doing a brisk business.

I had no idea.

They say this is the way living can begin to get away from you. You mean to do something. You have every intention. Yet one way or another it slides out of your grasp, a sudsy glass at the sink, and then the pin of it pricks you while you lie in bed one night: despite your best efforts, you have been remiss. Or perhaps certain important details in the lives of those around you have come close to escaping your notice—as in this second, when, raising my head to recite the phrase I am trying to learn by heart, *à bientôt, au revoir, à bientôt, au revoir,* I happen to glance over at my father and see it.

—What's that on your neck, Papa? I ask.

—My neck? he says distractedly.

He is busy sorting through his cards across from Mutti. Small round reading glasses balancing on the tip of his nose, two silver robins' eggs, he hears me but he doesn't hear me.

—Just above your collar. Did you hurt yourself?

In the dull yellow light, it appears to be a hard, shell-like blemish. A shiny brownish scab the length of two thumbnails. Papa reaches up and hunts the area with his fingertips.

Without letting his attention stray from his cards, he says:

—Nothing. It's nothing.

—Let me see, dear, offers Mutti.

She leans forward, her cards a patterned red-and-white peacock tail against her chest. Papa tugs down his collar. Mutti narrows her eyes. She extends her arm, semi-pointing, but can't quite reach the spot in question.

—I think you'll live, dear, she says.

I squint.

—Perhaps you cut yourself shaving.

Papa coughs into his fist, sound the ocher-yellow of toe-nails.

—Not that I recall, he says.

—There's nothing wrong with your father's neck, dear, says Mutti. Look for yourself. It's right as . . .

—Are we going to talk about my neck, asks Papa, tone shadowing, or are we going to play cards?

The charwoman lifts the wooden apple dish on the sideboard, flip-flaps the jittery white bat of her dust rag beneath it, and clunks it down again. We all stop what we're doing and look over at her. Her perspiration smells of garlic and fish heads. She tricycles on, oblivious, humming.

Then I have it: a Christmas carol.
That's what she's humming. A Christmas carol.
O Tannenbaum.
Yes.
That's it.

The holiday, I realize, sitting there, listening to the polar bear hum, somehow seems to have come and gone without any of us noticing.

margaret reading

The consequence of this last insight on the sister's part is to put us in mind of the fact that Uwe's sense of existential alienation is not limited to the clichés of early modernism, but rather extends to the very heart of Debord's assertion that *contemporary culture is the meaning of an insufficiently meaningful world, the effective dictatorship of illusion.* Or, to put it somewhat differently, Uwe's alienation is the essential reality of the pseudo-community produced by an industrialization of consciousness, a conurbation of spirit, a spectacular society of late capitalism whose goal is nothing less than an unending self-consumption every bit as virulent as the tubercles gnawing away at the mucus membranes of that young writer renting the flat below.

Cut off from each other and from themselves, caught in a real world become nothing more than real images proclaiming that whatever appears is good, whatever is good will appear, these bourgeoisie (the only revolutionary class, it would serve us well to keep in mind, that has ever been victorious beyond a doubt in their struggle for supremacy) treat those outside the pale as our culture always does the other—the mad, the elderly, the deviant, the diseased, the inventive. We conceal them in attics, in hospitals, in prisons, in back rooms, in basements, in ghettos.

We lock the doors on them, bar the windows, fetter the gates, commence straining to put them out of mind, for if we fail to the point of beginning to remember them, then we must commence forgetting ourselves.

the charwoman

First peek was a accident, like. Wanted to have meself a quick bit of up-and-down to see what all the fuss was about. You know how it is.

So one morning after everybody's gone out for the day I unlocks the door, pokes in me head, and there the little bugger is, shivering in that chair of his, not a pair of trousers in sight, slop bucket slooping over all greenish-brownish beside him.

Leaning his forehead against the windowpane, he is, squinting into the sleet coming down like as he might be near blind and can't hardly see it.

Wintry as a witch's teat in there. Stinks bloody dreadful, too. Like that oozy brown water at the bottom of a vase when you take out the dead flowers after waiting a week too long. Enough to turn a steel stomach.

Ain't deaf none, though. Hears me and *whoosh!* He's up rushing every which way, sixteen different kinds of bothered. Only, like I says, can't see none too good, so he barrels straight into the chest of drawers standing out there in the middle of the room like I don't know what. Goes down like a sack of rotten beets.

Just sort of lays there with his hands over his head, real still and all, 'cept for that shivering of his, like maybe I won't see him right in front of me on the carpet, fucking sorry piece of work.

But let me tell you something, boyo. I've cleaned up after my fair share of invalids. Legless Russians. Cancerous Jews.

And here's the what's what: there ain't nothing special about this one.

Miserable case, mind you, all scrotty, pongy, and skittish. Lump under his ear where his daddy sobered him up. Tufts of dust bunnies and cabbage shreds sticking to him. But it's the pink gash cross his belly what takes the cake. Skinny white worms long as me fingernail all a-wiggly inside there, like as they's struggling for a peek out the window, too.

A heart can't help go a little soft before such a sight, can it now, so I says, all merry, trying to raise his spirits:

—Come along, now, you old dung beetle! Why don't we get you washed up? Bet you'd fancy a bit of a spit bath about now, wouldn't you?

Truth is, it's sort of tricky to say whether he'd fancy one or not, him just laying there all shivery in front of me, hands over his head, face pink as a dog's tongue. Won't give me the bloody time of day, he won't, and I simply can't abide a man what won't give you the bloody time of day. Never know *what* a sod like that gots up his sleeve.

So I just gives him one of me good old long once-overs and out I goes, easy as one, two, don't do anything I wouldn't.

Only here's the curly one: I can't keep me distance. Human nature, is what it is. Couple of three days later there I is again, telling meself I'll just steal the quick fag. Break up the morning drudge. Easy enough forming a bad habit, innit. Slip inside. Lock the door behind me. Light up. Fold me arms. Lean back against the wall to take a load off the old trotters. Catch the cabaret.

Sometimes I chats him up. Sometimes I don't. We sort of gets used to each other being around and minds our own business. Least that's the way I figure it, till next thing I know the little bugger up and *charges* at me all piss-and-vinegary for no reason.

The *stones* on that prat.

The bloody *stones*.

But he don't scares me none. No, sir. I just lifts that chair of his over me head and says all spry like:

—*That's* the spirit! Let's have a bit of a laff now, shall we?

Well, he kind of peters out at that one, I can tell you.

Sizes me up, like.

Two of us have a bit of a stare-down, bit of a silent chinwag, if you know what I mean, till afters a time I speaks up and asks him:

—So that's all you got, then? That's the lot of it, is it? Well, you poor pathetic little Dublin University graduate, back you goes. Back you goes. *Get.*

Ever since, it's just like mother makes it, cuz here's what's what: you got to show them defectives right out of the gate. Otherwise they fancy they's all high and mighty. Better than the rest of us. You know how it is: me arm gets blowed off in the war and suddenly I'm like king of all I surveys.

Bollocks to that.

Though you got to admit he's cute as the dickens. In his own way, mind you. In his own way. Like one of them ribby pups with the mange what follows you home. Thinks he's hiding from you with nothing save his head covered, bare arse sticking up in the air like two scoops of vanilla ice cream.

Passes the time, is what I'm saying. I tells him all about me little buttercup in the state of Wyoming. Working a Laramie cathouse. Servicing the miners and sheepshaggers what live there. Makes a good wage doing it, too, thank you very much.

Writes me every month. Slips in the odd bill, too. A sweet one, she is. I ask the missus to reads her letters to me.

But here's the bit you can bank on, boyo, the bit you can take home for supper: seems no matter what they do, no matter what they don't, every mum and dad balls up their little ones at the end of the day.

Sure as eggs is eggs and no exceptions.

That's just how it is.

Every bloody one of them throws a spanner in the works one place or another. Only question is which gear's it going to be.

Yep: far as I can sees it, that's about the only one.

margaret reading

The wife's breathless dashes are emblematic of a larger gesture encompassing everything from Uwe's babble to the chambermaid's nervous backbroke ramble, the innumerable closed doors and sealed rooms in this muffled universe to the looming onto-epistemological silence of the natural disasters themselves: namely, how language finds its being in a perpetual incapacity to find its being, how the liquid in which we are dissolved fails to locate a moment's clarity, straightforwardness, or ease, continuously means more and/or other than what it ostensibly means to mean. Let us term this a *literary aphasia* and remind ourselves that its presence flies in the face of the almost legal precision (the abstract precision of austere German in which the Austro-Hungarian empire conducted its administrative affairs)—a careful articulation that signals a deep-structure belief in lucid communication—with which the narrative is constructed.

It is within this disjunctive, even desperate linguistic space that we may begin to locate Kafka's sense of hope.

mutti

But the hardest thing — you never expected it — is gathering together the family's jewelry — the Chinese box on the bureau — the velvet bag at the bottom of Papa's drawer — because you always pictured — for her wedding day — you always pictured how those pieces would look on her — our princess turning princess — the mother's pleasure at passing them down through the years — silver necklace — rhinestone robin — Papa's gold cufflinks for the prince — but we're different people now — why remember the people we aren't — so it's a short visit to the bearded Jew in the pawnshop — and even then — even with all that shame and a few extra marks — we won't be able to afford a good greasy leg of lamb — I remember how it — and so you wait till everyone is out for the day — charwoman busying herself in the kitchen — and you shrug on your coat your scarf your mittens — tell her you're popping down the block — cup of tea with a friend — back in an hour — at the door a second thought takes you unawares — less than a moment and it's in you — you hurry up the hall — into the living room — slip it off the wall — that one — hand on sword — listening to the charwoman clanking pots and pans — you take it down — leaving only the hook in its place — a bleached rectangle — little window that isn't there — tuck it under your coat — like that — angular past against your chest — and off you go — brief stop at the dustbin at the bottom of the stairs — then up the snowy street into the — into another day — pieces of yourself in your pocket — tight in your fist —

margaret

The breath mints in Margaret's mouth dissolve in a cool blue whish.

herrmann

Quick au lait at a café, quick grope in a mews, and off we go on our separate ways through the abominable snow.

Cricket says she won't indulge my fantasies again till we're man and wife.

Always the merry-andrew.

—Couldn't agree with you more, I reply, erection prodding the front of my trousers. I respect you and our relationship far too much to stoop to that sort of thing. A peck on the cheek, perhaps?

She measures me.

—Just one?

A peck it is, then, and off we trudge into the horrid weather, she back home to Mater and Pater and I to pick up a nelly for a little company near the castle.

Beautiful blond boy scrunched in a doorway four blocks away, trying to avoid the mess. Dark gray wooly roll-top two times too large for him. Matching wooly scarf and gloves. Cheeks pink as a Renoir after a bath.

No time at all and I'm en route to my flat to unwrap my present. Difficulty is, my bald-headed hermit has a mind of his own. Refuses to wait, the scamp. So I steer the three of us into a shoulder-wide gap between two buildings, behind some dustbins. Unbutton my coat, my fly, lean back against the wall, and go all dreamy. My beau may appear fifteen, but the lad possesses the delicate lips of a ten-year-old.

Few meters away pedestrians click-clack by. You can hear their voices. Young couple arguing. Two men talking trade. A convoy of chatty hausfraus on the prowl for tea and cakes.

Innocence, it dawns on me, standing there, is a wildly over-rated affair. It's criminality that takes the courage, the vision, broadens one's senses. Makes life start feeling like life.

My pup goes rabbity, what with all that noise about, but I reign him in, remind him of his business with my grip.

And that's when it hits me.

That's when I realize I'll marry her.

Funniest thing. You expect the muse to come round at the quiet, decorous, candle-lit hours, but as it happens the hussy pops by at the oddest instants. Right there in the midst of our lunch date she shows up with her memorandum. *I'll marry her.* Why not? Dowry shouldn't be anything to sneeze at. And with her and her money on my arm—well, it should be a fairly short climb up the rungs, shouldn't it?

Although, granted, living within one's means does represent a certain lack of imagination.

Nor do you want to rush into such matters. Enjoy one's youthful indiscretions while one can, particularly in one's mid-dle age. That said, it's most definitely time to drop round to meet the elders. Have ourselves a few good chats. Let them get to know the luminous joy called their new son-in-law.

Bring the missus a rose, the master a tale from the front. We can share war stories over cheroots, sherry, and his peg-leg, two old military men. And then, following dinner, ask the latter for his angel's diminutive claw. Explain the noble nature of my love, vow to provide his everything with the everything she and so forth.

Shouldn't take more than a month or two, once I put my

mind to it, although I shan't have to do the deed itself till I return from my next rotation. Leave a bachelor this summer. Return a reprobate next winter. Become a monk the following spring.

That should keep my beloved busy.

Wedding preparations, expectations, a handful of well-considered letters: the poor man's chastity belt.

And what self-respecting Pater could possibly say no to a chap cultivated and courteous as—

Ahhhhhhhhhhh . . .

The gurgle below.

The gag.

The extended surge of appre

margaret reading

ciate how the whole art of Kafka consists in forcing the reader
to reread. His endings, or his absence of endings, suggest explanations which, however, are not revealed in clear language
but require that the story be reread from another point of
view. Sometimes there is a double possibility of interpretation,
whence appears the necessity for two readings.

I should like to begin this essay by thanking, first, the German speakers in Bohemia for embracing Hitler's notion of a
greater Reich, and, second, the Communist regime for repress-
ing and nearly bankrupting my country for so many years.
Without these two forces, there is a good chance the world
would have forgotten the great writer Franz Kafka. They gave
us reason to remember him.

Kafka stood in our thoughts as a reminder of what these
others were not and could never be, and, therefore, of what we
could.

I recall as a seventeen-year-old youth—it was 1958—walking
through a foggy April morning down to the train station to
meet the troupe of Hungarian folk dancers who came to Prague
every spring to perform. What the authorities never compre-
hended was that those dancers smuggled tiny paperback cop-
ies of banned books into our country beneath their billowing
dresses. On this occasion, an underground edition of Kafka's
The Metamorphosis was among them.

That night I stayed up in my bed reading it for the first time, meeting this writer who dreamed of becoming a potato farmer or moving to Palestine, a rush of options sweeping through me. Although he did not write the longest work he completed while alive until November and December 1912, it had been growing within him since one summer evening in 1907, when he happened to see a play called *The Savage One* by a minor Yiddish author named Jacob Gordin. The play concerns an idiot son who remains locked in his room because he is frightened by his father's domestic tyranny.

The great irony of having had to read *The Metamorphosis* covertly and at some peril is how almost no one read the book freely and in complete safety when it originally appeared. Out of laziness and indifference, it was almost forgotten after the author's death. The Communists sought to erase the traces of it that survived, claiming it constituted the embodiment of bourgeois decadence.

Yet within a decade of my walk to that train, *The Metamorphosis* had become so much a part of the larger conversation that there existed film versions, play versions, and comic-book versions, humorous retellings, sad retellings, and simply odd ones, each a futile attempt to live closer to the Czech author for a brief time. Now it is taught in almost every high school classroom. There even exists a bad Broadway musical in which a mute Uwe is played by a mime with painted-on tears. And, of course, there are the thousands of books and essays like the one you are presently holding in your hands, each a modest demonstration of how much we care for a text that in toto amounts to fewer than seventy pages.

Each a means of saying thank you to all those who forced us to recollect by attempting to force us to forget.

All of Kafka is about history that had not yet happened. His sister Ottla would die in the camps, along with all of his kin. *Ungeziefer,* the word for insect that Kafka used for Uwe, is the same word the Nazis used for Jews, and *insect extermination* was one of their obscene euphemisms, as George Steiner has pointed out.

Poe's mind was round, fat, and white; Kafka's cubical, lean, and transparent.

What we are left with is the death or at least the dying of what we might call the Difficult Imagination—one that often finds itself accompanied by charges of exclusiveness, snobbery, and elitism leveled by faintly anxious readers at those disruptive, transgressive, nuanced texts dedicated in heterodox ways to revealing, interrogating, complicating, and, briefly, short-circuiting the comfortable narratives produced by dominant cultures committed to seeing such stories told and retold until they begin to pass for something like truths about aesthetics and the human condition.

I am not at all sure, as we find ourselves discussing this question of the avant-garde and accessibility with respect to Kafka, what we really mean by the latter term, since *accessibility* is one of those highly fraught, highly subjective words that, as Nabokov claimed of *reality,* should always appear between quotation marks. Nor am I clear about to whom a work should be *accessible*—a construction worker, a bus driver, an associate professor in the biology department in Bonn?

Nor do I understand why many people seem to believe texts in general should be more rather than less accessible.

Whatever we may think of when we use that word, texts in

general should be just the opposite. They should be *less* accessible, not more. Why? Because texts that make us work, texts that make us think and feel in unusual ways, texts that attempt to wake us in the midst of our dreaming, are more valuable epistemologically, ontologically, and sociopolitically than texts that make us feel warm, fuzzy, and forgetful.

When I speak of renewing the writing of the Difficult Imagination, I am referring to the renewal of a narratological possibility space in which we are asked continuously to envision the text of the text, the text of our lives, and the text of the world other than they are. This interzone of impeded accessibility is an essential one for human freedom. In it, everything can and should be considered, attempted, troubled. What is important about its products is not whether they ultimately succeed or fail (whatever we may mean when we say those words). What is important is that they come into being often and widely, because in them we discover the perpetual manifestation of Nietzsche's notion of the unconditional, Derrida's of a privileged instability, Viktor Shklovsky's ambition for art, and Martin Heidegger's for philosophy: the return, through complexity and challenge (not predictability and ease) to perception and contemplation.

Kafka's writing will always make one feel a little foolish, a little tongue-tied. One will find oneself standing there in a kind of baffled wonder that will insist upon a slightly new mode of perceiving, a slightly new way of speaking.

I am remembering, in a similar case involving one of Kafka's disciples, how I felt upon reaching the end of J. M. Coetzee's *Elizabeth Costello,* which commences by telling the life and obsessions of a contemporary writer in her late sixties by means of a series of lectures she gives and attends. It begins, that is to say, in the realm of psychological mimesis, but a psychological mimesis softly tweaked, askew, both by its structuring principle of those lectures as well as by a disquietingly flat prose style and the odd narratorial insertion (the passage of weeks, months, or years, for example, is covered by the abrupt phrase "We skip."). In the seventh of eight chapters, as the reader settles into these conventions, the novel unexpectedly leaves behind the universe of logical realism and Freudian depth-psychology, veering first into a highly textured meditation, still from the protagonist's point of view (although her presence drops back decidedly from it, while symbol swamps personhood), about the relationship between gods and mortals in a variety of mythological iterations, and then, in the final chapter, into a retelling of Kafka's

the charwoman

Can't say as I approve of how they's treating him, exactly, even if he ain't the brightest bulb in the lamp.

Yesterday the master of the house tells me start using the sickroom for storage. Put in the extra dining-room chair. Ash can they can't figure where it goes. Saves us a trip to the tip, he says.

Well, that's exactly what I does, thank you very much, cuz let me tell you something, boyo: I ain't getting paid for thinking, and I'll be goddamned if I'm going to start now.

Still, a person can't help noticing. Can't help taking things in. And I takes in plenty.

Like, for instance, how that good-for-nothing daughter of theirs cares more for macking her military man what never shows his face around here than spending ten with her own flesh and blood. Bleeding *disgraceful,* is what it is. Pushes leftovers into his room with her foot just like as she's nudging along a bowlful of dogshite.

Truth is, it's tricky to say whether he'd eat any more if he had it. I seen him suck at a mouthful of pap for ages what he spits into his palm and wipes most of it across the walls. Upchucks little cat-pukes of the rest like as he can't keep the mouse down.

Ain't as much fun as he used to be, neither. Once in a blue moon he'll make the old stab at charging me. Open his gob wide, trying to bring up a hiss. Only nothing comes out save a squeak of dry air. You can sees the blisters all over the inside. Heart ain't into it none.

Thin as a streak of piss and twice as knackered.

Don't even bother reaching for that chair no more when he starts up, I don't. Just stares at him, smoking, though every so oftens I can't helps meself. You know how it is. Cracks a smile, lowers meself onto me haunches, offers him a bit of a scratch under the chin.

—Sometimes a body don't want to overstay his stop-by, I whispers to him all kind, like, scratching. Ain't polite, you know, you old dung beetle.

He seems to enjoy that.

Leaning into me fingers and whatnot.

grete

It is precisely the sort of day it should be: sky a creamy smear of promise, pedestrians flooding the cobbled banks of the river, pushing prams, wielding balloons, tugging leashed terriers, licking ice-cream cones, strolling arm in arm with dates or hand in hand with tots, almost every flushed face upturned to the damp heat. A few black automobiles inch among them like fat beetles searching for scraps.

I watch them from beneath my parasol in a dory drifting on the muddy current, suspended in the lime melody of Herrmann's aftershave, water slipslapping on all sides. Between us an open wicker picnic basket. Brown nub of French bread. Quarter block of cheddar. Half-empty bottle of white wine beside two long-stemmed glasses hazy with fingerprints.

It is precisely the sort of day it should be, the one I would have imagined had I been asked to imagine it in advance. Farther downstream, a darkly varnished schooner at dock, sails furled, masts and rigging competing with the surrounding church spires, a slow flat ferry crowded with passengers plying from bank to bank, and, farther still, floating bars and cafés whose reappearance announces the arrival of the season.

Leaning back on my elbows, I shut my eyelids and live for a few breaths in the blush behind them: distant chatter, human hum, oily fish, and tar on the breeze. When I open them again, Herrmann is holding up the chardonnay as an offering.

—Another glass?

—I couldn't. If I become any more content, I'm afraid I might simply glide away.

—And tell me: what would be so awfully wrong with that? I can't think of a lovelier picture. You gliding up and up over the city.

A row of teenagers dangle their legs off the far bank beneath a tree fuzzily chartreusing. Behind them a beer garden. They are passing a clear bottle back and forth, laughing. A ginger-colored cat perches owlish on one's lap, meditating.

—Half a glass, I say. Not a single drop more.

—Brilliant.

He adds as an afterthought, pouring:

—Otherwise there could be no toast.

—Toast?

—In celebration of your answer, naturally.

He presents me with my drink.

Our glasses chinkle.

—Whatever to? I ask.

—To the favor I am about to ask you. Cheers. Mmmmm. Delicious, isn't it? Will you marry me?

My heart tugs askew.

He scratches his beard, head bobbing lower.

—You absolutely must, you know. I won't take no for an answer. Consider yourself formally shanghaied. You're my prisoner. We shan't touch shore again until I have my yes. I have all week, I should mention, although I suspect it might get rather nippy at night.

Then he unveils the fairy-tale smile of his that makes me feel I am falling and falling and falling and falling and falling.

grete

Twenty minutes, and our dory bumps the pier. A large man with a broken nose and black knit cap reaches down to steady it. Herrmann steps out, turns to offer me his hand with a small, suave bow. I rise charily, parasol nervous above me; then he has my wrist and my forearm and is hoisting me up.

The blast lifts and jerks me sideways. Its shockwave comes as a silver luminosity. The day flies to pieces, and the footpath leaps into my shoulder.

The atmosphere grainy with dust and sparkling flakes.

I am blind.

I am deaf.

Then I am nothing at all.

margaret reading

parable "Before the Law," in which Elizabeth rather than Kafka's man from the country seeks entrance in vain, not from the quotidian world into the law, but from a purgatorial in-between place into some beyond-region—possibly heaven itself. The book ends with a brief, cryptic postscript that takes the form of an epistle from another (or is it somehow the same?) "Elizabeth C." (Elizabeth, Lady Chandos), this one quite possibly on the verge of madness, written on 9/11 . . . not in 2001, as we might expect, but in 1603, the year the English Renaissance begins its concluding with the death of Elizabeth I.

With that, everything we have just read drifts into suspension. Is the narrative supposed to add up to the hallucinations of a seventeenth-century woman? A twentieth-century woman imagining from beyond the grave, or on her way to it? A serious postulation of cyclical rebirth or eternal recurrence? An ironic one? Or, more likely, a text not about character and mimesis at all, but rather about a series of philosophical and literary problems, an investigation into a novel ripped open as unpredictably as our culture was on that glistery blue September day, a universe and a universe of discourse exploring the conditions of their own self-perplexing existence?

But one might rightfully ask oneself: can the Difficult Imagination's project ever hope for something resembling success—however we may define *that* word?

The answer is, of course, absolutely

grete

—*Are you all right?* someone is asking above me. *Are you all right?*

My tongue tastes tinny with blood.

Each breath is a thick labor of soot and sulfur.

I return to myself gradually.

Nearby, people are moaning from deep within their voice boxes. Fire wagons clang in the distance. A panicked woman shouts out someone's name.

Her husband? Her little boy?

—Open your eyes, someone else is saying in my ear. He sounds calm, in charge, like someone you can trust. His warm rough palm rests on my jaw. Show me you're all right. Open your eyes.

I do as I am told, and the first thing I see through the gray dizziness is a man's trousered leg hanging off an overturned park bench.

The upper half of his torso on the cobblestones.

A once well-dressed old woman sits on the ground beside it, knees to her chest, dress in tatters, rocking, a shiny red trickle from her right ear.

I understand without understanding.

This is how it happens.

This is how the natural disasters arrive.

margaret reading

not. And maybe. Staging the inaccessible is an always-already futile project. And an always-already indispensable one. Its purpose is never a change, but rather a changing that will occur—if it occurs at all—locally. That is, writing of the Difficult Imagination cannot generate a macro-revolution (what art can, after all?), but rather a necklace of micro-ones: nearly imperceptible, ahistorical clicks in consciousness that come when one meets a surprising, illuminating, challenging fictive thought experiment.

What else could any of us ask for from a narrative?

Or, Carole Maso: we write *wholeheartedly into our own obsolescence, our own obscurity—a place at once tender and absurd and fierce.*

the charwoman

It's a real knock, like, the way it comes down. Everybody jumpy as them blind mice in front of the farmer's wife, and the food supplies going all to hell.

Not that there was much to begin with. Not with the war. But now looks at us. If this don't bugger all.

I pop over to the market one morning to pick up the makings for supper and find a few soggy potatoes left on the vegetable carts. Next morning them's gone as well. Soon the bakeries are filling out their bread with sawdust, all quiet-like, like maybe nobody'll notice.

Day the queer-looking meat starts showing up at the butcher's, people start remarking how we ain't seen as many dogs nor pigeons as usual. Enough to makes you wish we ain't been so up-and-at-'em with them rats.

Then the animals at the zoo goes missing, one by one.

Still, we got plenty of drinking water from the city fountains—if everybody weren't all collywobbles about drinking it. Matter of time before the poisoning begins, they says. So they takes the river water instead. You can imagine the outcome of that little pearl.

Only maybe they got a point. Blokes what can sneak into a city, take a proper retard, strap a bomb to him, and set him loose in a Sunday crowd can do pretty much anything they pleases. And the poor defective not even twelve years old. The very idea of it.

Not seeing them anywheres don't help none. You hears the explosions. A tram here. A theater there. Sometimes on the other side of the river. Sometimes two blocks away. Sometimes you hears how one of them defectives starts screaming and waving as they's running toward a café. How people tries getting out of their way. How some do and some don't.

Them horses standing all by their lonesome in the town square every morning in the rain, mouth-sized bites taken from their flanks.

Electricity comes and goes.

Rubbish collects along the pavement like the whole city's moving and has put their bags out to be hauled away.

But thing is, they never *shows* themselves. That's the part that starts working on a body. Make a stab at getting on with your business, but you can *feels* them. Right down inside your joints. They ain't there, only they are.

Ain't long neither before rumors flies how some women is offering themselves up for a couple heads of cabbage or jar of apple preserves. You see little notes stuck on lampposts, walls, store windows. Boys, too. Girls not more than ten.

It don't matter none. Families do what they gots to. No apologies from anybody on that score.

Only just about the time you get to thinking this is about as low as things is likely to drops, the cold snap blows in from the north. Bitter as a well-digger's arse. Kind that makes your hands feel like as refrigerated meat. Season's coal near gone. Ain't no more coming. So people takes to sawing limbs off the trees along the streets and in the cemeteries and parks. Breaking up furniture. Sorting through the tip like a bunch of gypsy beggars.

I drops by the flat to tidy some of an evening and comes

across the master squatting in front of the stove. Feeding it pages from this book with a picture of a bug on the cover. Little stack of other books already going real good inside. Ain't much heat, though. More like the thought of heat. Don't even wish me a good evening, he don't.

And when I show up this morning, *whuff,* they's taken on lodgers. Three of them. Sods ain't never smiled a day in their sorry lives. That's a fact. Move through the flat in step like they's part of the same spider in shabby black. *Scholars,* like. That's the word. They's scholars, thinking all their ideas and whatnot.

Nothing's too clean for them kind. Brings their own bedding. Wipes the rims of their glasses with their handkerchiefs before drinking. And dinner? What a laff. Missus shows up at the living-room door with a nice dish of jackdaw she's paid through the nose for, only them sods bends over when it's set down before them sniffing at it like a pack of bearded dogs.

Leader twists off a drumstick, licks it, checking if it's cooked right or it gets sent back to the kitchen.

Family swallows the last bit of bleeding pride and commences taking meals in the kitchen. Sometimes you can hear them going at each other about money whilst the lodgers chow in the living room without a solitary word passing amongst them, spit and teeth working all slobbery.

Master and missus got to give up their rightful bedroom and move into that daughter's to make space, too. Daughter takes to sleeping in the living room. Tries not to disturb them what wastes their evenings reading, but it ain't easy.

Let me tell you something, boyo. Them lodgers? Them lodgers can kiss me bloody Christian bum, going about acting like some bunch of hoity-toity snoots.

I swear, I'll be a goddamned Chinaman.

margaret

—*Are you all right?* someone asks above her.

Margaret must have zoned out, sunk so deep into her book that she lost all sensation of *being* anywhere. Now it dawns on her someone is talking. Someone is asking her a question.

She returns to herself gradually, and, embarrassed, as if caught doing something mildly indecent, she half-revolves in her seat and looks up.

That corpulent security guard from the main hall is standing in front of her, his dangly arms striking her as a bit too short. The image of a podgy thalidomide child arrives behind her forehead. She wonders what her face must be doing, because his, jowly and stubble-shadowed, is adolescently expectant.

—Oh, she says. Hi. It's you. Hi.

—Sorry to bother you, he says, lifting those odd arms from his sides a few centimeters. But, em, I read here on break, too, sometimes, and, so. I couldn't help drifting over. To ask. Did you fancy it, then?

He nods at the dark green volume with gold lettering winged open in her lap.

Margaret decides she would describe the thinning wedge of his receding hair as the color of oatmeal mush.

—Afraid I'm not as far as it appears. Thought some of the essays in back might help. Regrettably. But yes. Yes, I do. Quite a lot so far. I haven't read anything like it. It's very good . . . in some fairly ominous and hard-to-articulate way.

She grins and in the middle of grinning becomes intensely self-conscious. Margaret isn't used to talking about books. The act makes her feel pretentious and artsy. Sneaking a glance around her, she sees it is as she feared: other patrons have begun taking note.

—Exactly, the security guard says, casually picking up the slack. Right. It all seems so . . . *strange,* I suppose, is the word, innit? Eccentric. Like those lodgers and their memory work. Or the, what . . . the abstract creepiness of the natural disasters. You don't really know what's going to happen . . . only not in the sense that you don't really know what's going to happen in an American film, but in the sense that you don't really know what's going to happen in your own life.

The security guard chirp-laughs, and the head of a young librarian with short carefully mussed reddish-copper hair pops up from behind a row of reference books and shushes him, then, face emotionless, drops out of sight again on an invisible lift.

—It's, em, Timothy, by the way, he whispers, cringing, turning back to Margaret. Isn't it funny why you like a particular book? Why one book stays with you rather than another? I used to assume it had something to do with the book being bad or good or whatever. But now I'm pretty sure it has to do with it making you feel at the end of the day like you like to feel. Happy, sad, baffled, excited.

—I hadn't, actually. Stopped to think about it. But yes. I see what you . . .

—It's like people read to find out what they already know. Only they don't know they already know. Like maybe they're trying to find missing bits of themselves. And, so. Any chance I might . . . em, you know, interest you in a cup of coffee or something? I've still got most of an hour, and the museum café is quite nice, if you don't mind many things wrapped in plastic. Forks. Cakes. Small children. Maybe we could . . .

—Oh. No. Thank you. No.

Timothy's arms give up trying to levitate him off the bluegray carpet.

Holding up her volume as some kind of proof, Margaret explains:

—The thing is, I'm too close to the end to stop right now. I've got to find out how it all turns out.

—Oh, right. Well, no worries. I, em . . . right. I suppose I should push off, then. Get a bit of reading done myself. He holds up the light blue paperback in his hand: *Elizabeth Costello*. Enjoy the homestretch. You'll never guess the ending, but in retrospect it'll make perfect sense.

Timothy turns to leave, and Margaret's heart tugs askew.

She catches herself.

—But this evening? she adds. At nine? There's this book club thing going on? Over in Camden Town? Nothing very flash, I'm sure. Only I've never been, and, well, I was just wondering . . .

the three lodgers

We appear for dinner at six o'clock. This is our plan. We take our positions at the table and bow our heads. We say a brief prayer for our city under siege. *May the natural disasters depart. May they take their bombs and their hatred with them. May the spring of hunger come to an end before another month has passed. May we remain strong in our hearts and may food always find us. Amen.*

We say this prayer, although we do not believe in it. We would like to, but we cannot. We say it because this is what we do. Then we clean our forks and knives with our handkerchiefs. Small, vigorous, circular rubbing motions. Dog meat is gray and stringy. It catches easily in the teeth. There is no gravy to help it down. We have asked for gravy every evening and still there is none. It has not been easy for us.

Mealtimes are for memorizing what we have memorized through the day. We eat and recall. Since the invasion, our work has become more vital. When we conclude it, we will slip out of the city under cover of darkness and cross the border into free territory. Perhaps next month. Perhaps next year. We are in no hurry. We will spend the remainder of our days remembering. Manuals. Poems. The lists of those who have perished here. If the natural disasters leave, we will return and recollect for others.

We eat and then we finish eating. In unison we pat our mouths with napkins and wipe our hands. We wipe our hands again. We work toothpicks through our dental intricacies. We ask for our newspaper and our cigar. We are entitled to both. We have an agreement. We share them among ourselves. Smoking and reading, we learn by rote what is happening. How resources run down. How bad becomes worse. How a zeppelin went up in billowing flames yesterday evening over the river. Little fiery droplets of crew fell from the sky. When we reach safe haven, we will be able to report how our city lived its final days.

It is triage, only with history. Over the years, we have learned each memory is not a picture, not a miniature movie, but a collage that arrives in multihued flecks. A sound from here in the brain. An image from there. An emotion from somewhere else. Put them together, and you have something like the past. Not the past itself, but something like it.

We read and we smoke and then we become aware of the violin music washing in from the kitchen. It is neither good playing nor bad. It is simply playing. A piece by Bach in D minor. *Partita Number Two.* Variations on a theme. We can say no more. We lift our heads to take in the melody. At length we push back our chairs and move down the hallway.

We remain outside the kitchen door. We commence tapping our toes to test the rhythms' accuracy for our records. Evidently this alerts those on the other side to our presence, because the landlord calls out:

—Is the violin playing disturbing you, gentlemen? It can be stopped at once. Would you like me to stop it?

ραρα

—On the contrary, responds the middle lodger. Could not Miss Samsa perhaps come play in the living room? Surely it would be much more convenient and comfortable for us all.

Chest enlarging with pride, as if he himself were the musician, The Father meets the eyes of his wife and daughter and shoos them on their way, his hand a tiny whiskbroom, responding:

—Oh, yes, certainly! Certainly! Why don't you gentlemen have yourselves seats? We shall be along directly.

A brisk flutter, a tugging down of sleeves, an arranging of rumpled clothing and ruffled hair, and The Father is carrying Grete's music stand, leading the way, his wife two steps behind him with a sheaf of tunes, his daughter three with her instrument. The Father hurries, marveling: who in the world would have thought it? Those lessons are finally paying off. Here, at this age, at this distant point on the river, I am experiencing one of what they call *the hidden rewards of parenthood*.

In the living room, warmed by an unconvincing book fire, everyone takes his or her place. The Father presents chairs to the lodgers but himself remains standing by the entrance, right hand thrust between two buttons of his uniform, a white-haired, mustachioed Napoleon. Grete plucks at the strings of her violin, tuning. The middle lodger offers The Father's wife a chair from the dining room table. Flustered, unaccustomed to dealing with boarders, she leaves it where it was set, the consequence being that, when she settles, she finds herself balancing precariously on a single unforgiving corner. The Father opens his mouth to reprimand her, and then, considering decorum, thinks better of it. He files away a mental note to address her concerning this matter after everyone has retired for the evening. Now he will act in a manner befitting others of his place.

Grete begins.

There is silence, there is music, and the music is magic.

At once The Father's eyes brim with tears. Assuming three marks for an hour's lesson, he calculates, vision blurring, heart balmy, and one lesson per week each year, minus Christmas and Easter, over the course of—how many years was it? Seven at least. No. More. Quite possibly more. He will have to consult with Mutti about the particulars. Regardless, an initial invest-ment of barely one thousand marks has resulted in nothing less than this splendid number.

Look at her fingers move. The grace. These things, this min-ute, this feeling of satisfaction are a steal for such an outlay of capital. And look at Mutti, sitting there a queen (her odd pos-ture on the chair's brink notwithstanding), nearly as intent on savoring what their daughter has wrought as The Father him-self. Grete has matured, grown up. Thank the Lord her wounds are minor and healing. At the end of the day, she is likely to come through this abominable bombing business with nothing more than a few indistinct scars above her left eye, an indistinct wobble in her step, eligible as ever, perhaps even more so. Who, taking one thing with another, isn't drawn to the negligible flaw, the blemish, God's little kisses that make us who we are?

Plumped with gratification, he shifts his attention to the

lodgers—to the leader puffing away at his stumpy cigar in The Father's easy chair, bluegray nebulae rising around him, to the other two broomhandle-backed on the sofa, taking their pleasure stoically, like the Finnish—and The Father dares for the shortest of instants to entertain a half-thought: *one of them, one of them, yes, quite possibly—who, after all, is to say?*

mutti

They don't — oh dear — you can tell right away can't you — they don't care for it one whit — two shakes and they've had enough — off they go to the window in a pack — whispering among themselves — cigar smoke hissing from their noses like — like a band of devils — you can see it — downbent heads — the way they were expecting something more — and yet she is playing so wonderfully — face atilt — beautiful eyes tracing beautiful notes — it's mortifying beyond words — and now — oh dear — *Mister Samsa!* cries the middle one turning — me gawking in disbelief in the direction he's pointing — and how did *that* happen — how did *he* get out — it's almost too much to bear — one person can only stand so — the charwoman must have — the music breaks off in mid-bar — Grete's eyes aflame — the lodgers looking on with — with nothing more than mild interest at first — calculating — that's what they're doing — and *him* working himself slowly forward — covered with fluff — dried splinters of old food — oh dear God in heaven — it's a scandal — how could he — *Mister Samsa!* shouts the middle one — *what is the meaning of this?* — *we demand an explanation* — waving his arms above his head — *we demand one this very second* — and Papa rushing toward them — arms outspread — a great blue bird flapping on the beach — trying to calm them — ease them back toward their room — give them a moment to compose themselves — and now *him* stepping forward too — toward his sister —

but Grete ducks — ducks and rushes around him before he can — shoving her violin into my hands — plunging down the hall — past Papa — past the others — into the lodgers' room — to set their bed in order for them — and poor Papa — he forgets himself completely — who can blame him — drives the lodgers on — stubborn cattle — drives them on — till at the bedroom door — I knew it — the middle one stops — stamping his foot in frustration — everyone coming up short — *I beg to announce* — he says — indignant — all superior in that way of theirs — *because of the disgusting conditions prevailing in this household — we are hereby forced to give notice — this is simply unacceptable — what we have endured* — can't believe my ears — *needless to say we refuse to pay a single pfennig — not a single one — on the contrary — we find ourselves compelled to consider bringing legal action for damages* — I see the police knocking at our door — the looks in our neighbors' eyes — and then they are gone — door slamming behind them — and instead of attempting to plead — what good would that do — Papa's shoulders simply slump — his head drops — and back he comes into the living room — shambling — crumpling wordless into his chair — right past *him* just standing there — how could he — oblivious — as though everything is — not even acknowledging the noise — the angry twang of Grete's violin — such a butterfingers — slipping off my lap — striking the floor — shocked at the world — shocked and appalled —

grete

I feel lost just by standing here, my family happening around me.

In the dead air, the hanging moment, I look over at Papa caved into himself in his easy chair, how he stares at heaven through his closed eyelids, rubbing his chest through his unbuttoned jacket.

I look over at Mutti trying to net her breath, gawping at the carpet in front of her, how she gives the impression of someone who has just been stabbed but can't quite take in the fact.

Then I look over at him, eyes pinched shut, hands cupped over ears, knees bent, his little wobbly bits hanging down like withered graywhite packages of grief.

My zombie brother is somewhere else.

Traveling.

Perhaps you cannot blame somebody for being himself, but having to look at him right now feels like nipping the inside of my own cheek.

—Listen, I say. Listen. This is a difficult thing for us to admit, I know. We have tried and tried to care for it, put up with it as far as is humanly possible. We have been the most faithful of families. No one can reproach us in the slightest for our efforts. But things have not gone well. Look at us. I'm sorry to say it, but we all know this deep inside.

There follows the long stillness of an unlighted corridor, broken by Papa saying to no one, rubbing:

—She's right, you know.

Mutti remains mute.

Sometimes I wonder, looking from one to the other, what family is for. You live in one all your life only to discover yourself in a room like this, and yet all you have in common with these people is the color of your eyes, the slant of your nose.

I wait another few spiky seconds, then push on:

—Otherwise . . . I don't mean to sound theatrical . . . but otherwise this will be the death of us. It will. How can we possibly work as hard as we do, day in, day out, yet have to face this added torment? The time we have sat with it, nursed it, cleaned up its mess, made all manner of compromises in our own lives to make it more comfortable. The situation is quite intolerable.

More corridor.

More stillness.

I know no matter what happens I shall always remember these minutes.

I push on:

—We must decide between us and it. This is what I have to say. I don't want to, yet I have to. We must make a decision.

Opening his puffy, saggy eyes, glancing over in my direction without turning his head, Papa asks:

—But, sweetheart, what can we do?

—This is the burden God gave us, Mutti says, gawping, hands flaccid sea creatures washed up into her lap. He wouldn't ask us to carry it if He didn't think we were up to the task.

—If only it could understand us, says Papa, speaking more to himself than to us. If only that, then perhaps we could come to some sort of agreement. But as things stand . . .

—As things stand . . . Mutti parrots.

I look at her. I look at Papa. At Papa, at her.

The things the natural disasters can do to you.

In the end, family exists for no reason other than leaving it. This is the secret everyone keeps from you. People behave as if it were the opposite. Sooner or later everyone discovers he or she is wrong.

I wait until I cannot wait any longer, then say with some finality:

—It must go. I'm sorry. It must. We have tried to negotiate. Share. We have attempted to accommodate it every way possible. Yet it refuses to reciprocate. It doesn't even *try*. It wants the whole apartment to itself.

I detect movement out the corner of my eye and turn to see what is going on. While we have been conversing, it has commenced a protracted rotation. We all cease what we are doing to watch it as if watching an egg beginning to hatch. It is positioning itself to withdraw toward its room, but its movements are jerky, fitful, stiff, a slow-motion comedian in a silent movie. Eyes pinched tight, hands over ears, knees bent, it is shuffle-feeling its way along in the caricatured motions of an elderly blind man, muttering to itself:

—Because the voice on the radio is filled with hands, because of that, minutes come at us, timeflakes drifting down, *bam, bam, bam*, I shaved his head, she powdered his brain, my favorite part being the scarf, the long black ribbon of dreams, but it must have blown overboard, the waves rocking me, and up we go into the night, dread in our hearts, shooting all around us, up we go, lads, into the weather, where did it come from, turning the dial, we can't pick up a station, only the clock ticking in the middle of my neck, *bam, bam, bam,* let me touch your forehead, please, like this, so I can see the future through your skull, the way the cold eats thoughts on the balcony, your shell itching, do what you might, has someone perhaps seen my legs, I once had so many, tomorrow being just like today, only much, much longer, because the pasture never stops, it goes on and on until the very beginning, history gathering at your feet, call it idea activity in the nonspecific landscape, call it the impossible science of the unique being, quiet as a *bam, bam, bam,* call it the moving ability, here I go, into the weather, quit mucking about, lads, because there are moments, we all know it, when the wig has to come off . . .

We all observe its uneven progress in melancholy silence.

At the door, it sticks out its arms before it in order better to navigate sightless through the opening.

Once it crosses the threshold, I hurry over and shut the door behind it. Throw the lock. The unlighted corridor grows and grows. I am the only one in it. I lean my forehead against the cool painted surface, reeling, trying extraordinarily hard to change myself into the air surrounding me.

I want to say I open the door again. I want to say I enter his room, drag him off his chair, commence strangling him on the floor. I don't remember. I am not strangling him now. He is lying on his side, holding his throat. I am on my knees beside him. I am outside his room, leaning my head against the cool painted surface of the door.

the charwoman

Well, you can just pictures the state I'm in, what with the rain banging down in black sheets and buckets this morning, and me there, wet to the bone and not even a bloody fire to greet me as I lets meself in.

Not even that, and me puddling all over the foyer like a cur what ain't been housebroke yet.

Let me tell you something, boyo. Growing old in this world ain't for the skittish. Course, the other choice ain't no better, so off I goes about me chores in the half-light, setting the kitchen in order, moving up the hallway into the living room.

That daughter of theirs snoring on the sofa. How come *she* gets the lay-back in life while all's I get is me long-handled broom and an apron full of the mullifubbles? Look at her. Purple shame, innit. That ain't working. That's taking up somebody else's air.

Looking at her, it ain't long before I figures time for a quick fag. Give a top of the morning to the chucklehead. Only when I have meself a peek inside his room, first thing I makes out is his slop bucket's empty as his overturned chair.

Now where'd he get himself off to? Ain't like him, not taking in the view. I squints into the dawn that don't want to be dawn yet. Stench so sodding sharp and greasy, makes all the others up to now seem a flaming picnic in the park.

Then I catches sight of him over by the desk. Not under it,

mind you. On the floor aside it. Curled up like a bug what's been touched by a match.

Doing it to get me goat, I figures. You know how it is. Haven't been dropping by much as I used to. So I steps over and gives him a bit of the prod with me broom. Tickling, like. Reckon it might rouse him from the sulks. Only he don't do nothing. So I pokes at him harder. Things don't feel on the level. Broom handle seems to be pushing into a crumpled-up ball of newspaper.

I squint harder, get down on me haunches to have a closer look-see . . . and that's when it starts sinking in. His straggly hair hanging all over his face. Wide-open mouth dry-spittle-rimmed. Parts of him I can't even make out no more what's skin and what ain't, there being so much shite clinging to him.

Squatting, knees crackly, having meself a good up-and-down, I listen to the rain glugging through the drainpipes outside and let go a long low whistle. The way some things turn out. A body knows and a body don't know right up till the last, but the train station always comes as a surprise on the journey. *That's it?* you asks yourself, all stumped, feeling the carriage slowing down. *That's the whole bloody bit?* Scenery sure do speed by, only no matter what you do all of a sudden there you is, pulling in.

I don't let it get the best of me. First hundred years the hardest. But it makes me dizzy. So much so, I got to have meself a sit-down. Cross me legs and waits till the minutes start coming back. Then I shakes it off and out the door I goes, calling:

—*Hallo! Hallo! You can come out now! You can come out!*

Makes a path straightaway to the daughter's room, where the master and missus are holed up in bed, and I gives a good *rappity-rap* on the door with me broom handle. Ain't no answer, and it ain't locked, so I swings it open and gives a loud yelp into the stuffy nighttime in there.

Curtains pulled tight. Can't see a bleeding thing, hardly. Then there's a slapdash commotion beneath the blankets. Master rises like as a new island in the India Ocean. Props himself up in bed, massaging his face with both paws, trying to place himself in all the nothing.

Takes him a while to get his bearings.

You know how it is.

—Well now, he says after a few thousand years, croaky voice rolling out of the murk. Well now, well now, well now. I suppose at least that's behind us, then, isn't it?

the three lodgers

Every morning the same, even this one, even our last. If we have asked that charwoman not to slam doors once, we have asked her twenty times. No one can enjoy a moment's rest after she and her racket arrive.

And here she is again, bellowing down the hallway.

This flat has turned out to be no better than a common whorehouse.

There is no fighting it. There is nothing to do. We rise slowly, we wash, we dress, our hope of sleep behind us. We proceed to the dining room table. It is six o'clock. Outside a blustery downpour. Inside light the color of oyster slobber. The bedding is still bunched on the sofa, although the daughter is nowhere in sight. The table is still unset. We cannot believe our eyes. All this din, and the house remains in shambles. It will be hard for us to the very last.

In the middle of it stands the charwoman, lone Holstein in a pasture, broom raised in one hoof.

—Where is our breakfast? we demand, hands in the pockets of our coats.

She raises her other hoof to her lips and jabs her broom in the general direction of his bedroom. We look. The door is open again. After everything that has happened, the door is open again. To let a son like that have free reign. What kind of household is this? But the charwoman is insistent. She jabs her broom at us. She jabs her broom in the general direction of his bedroom. We must have a closer look inside. This is what she is telling us. Wary, we do as she indicates.

From the doorway, nothing appears out of the ordinary. We turn and consult the charwoman. She jabs at us. She jabs at the open door. We sidle through. Everything is as it always has been: jumble of unused furniture, linen mounds, pillows, newspapers, magazines, ash bins, slop bucket, even a filthy blond wig on the filthy tan carpet. The room isn't a room. But we are used to this sight. This is what happens when rules let go.

Initially we mistake him for another swell of litter. Then we see our mistake. He is lying on his side by the desk, knees to chest, fists tucked under chin, daylight increasing around him in one long, slow breath.

Moving closer, we begin our recollection work. What is left of him puts us in mind of something of tremendous age. Ancient pottery that has lain on the ocean floor for thousands of years, caked with lint clots, small gray goose-down feathers, toothpicks, slivers of rotted cabbage, shiny blisters of yellowish fat, desiccated flies, a pencil eraser, paint chips, a fine diaphanous fungus, greenish smears of dried excrement.

The room does not smell of rot.

The room smells of blood.

—*Get away from him!* bellows the landlord's voice behind us.

We jump and pivot.

He is wearing that ridiculous uniform of his, his slovenly wife on one arm, his slovenly daughter on the other. They appear to have been crying. Their eyes are puffy and red. But they are not crying anymore.

—I *beg* your pardon, we say. We are merely . . .

—*Leave my house at once!* The *gall!* The *GALL! Snooping around like this! And in the very hour of our wretchedness! How DARE you! Get out! GET OUT THIS VERY SECOND!*

We study this madman. We weigh our options.

—Whatever in the world do you mean?

—*I mean precisely what I say. LEAVE. MY. HOUSE.*

And, with that, he advances toward us, the two women still in tow.

—*Well!* we say, attempting to maintain our composure. Then by all means we shall be going. We shan't need to be asked twice.

Displaying the greatest possible solemnity, we stride by the preposterous trio and down the hallway. In the foyer, we retrieve our hats from the rack, our sticks from the umbrella stand. We take our time in order to show these people that we are not afraid of them. But we do not take too much.

Finished, we quit the flat, saying over our shoulders as we depart:

—Once you have seen fit to collect yourselves, we shall be back for our . . .

—*LEAVE!* the master of the house bays at the ceiling.

As we descend, passing a pimply-faced butcher's boy on his way up with a tray on his head, the landlord and his women appear on the landing. They are there to keep an eye on us, make sure we depart without causing further trouble.

On every floor, their graywhite faces come into view momentarily and then disappear again.

Gradually, they rise away.

Gradually, they become another occurrence of memory.

the butcher boy

You can smell it as they pass. Yids. She's one, too, Mrs. Kling-hoffer. Everywhere nowadays. Mr. Meiwes told me step on it. No dallying. Then straightaway back to the store. She pays in bracelets and rings. Finest pups for her. Plenty left, if you know where to look. Follow the bankers home. Wait for dusk out back. That's the way it's done. Open the gate to the garden. Kneel down in the alley. Bring out the bone from beneath your coat. They try to refuse it at first, only they can't. You can see it in their eyes, trying to work through the risks. Their bodies do them in. Lower their heads. Come up at you sideways with their tails tucked down. Stay still till they start sniffing the knuckle joint. Babytalk them. Then grab them by the scruff. They try to jerk back. Hold on. Bring around the hammer. *Ark!* they go. *Ark! Ark! Ark!* Legs back-peddling. Teeth snapping. That's when you hit them in the mouth. The snout. Second they lose their balance it's over. Shuddering on the cobblestones, they don't stop running, only they do it on their sides. Trick is not letting up. Let up, you can lose a finger. Trick is not seeing them but the coins in Mister Meiwes's palm. Then the soggy noises become peaceful noises. Nobody cares what you're doing. That isn't how it goes these days. Stuff them in your burlap sack. Walk them over to Mr. Meiwes. Cats to the Catholics, dogs to the Yids. *Money always buys the right amount of violence.* That's what Mr. Meiwes says. What are those three looking at now? Stupid old git. Man-servant dawdling with his maids. What's so fucking funny?

mutti

Everybody all at once laughing out loud — oh dear — can you imagine — funniest thing in the world — the way they take the steps — two at a time — and that butcher boy — snotsmear across his cheek and not a clue — because it's ours again you see — hasn't been for ages but now it is — like dropping in a lift — tummy all light and alive — so we drift back inside — to our bedroom — *come in beside us darling* I say to Grete — *come in* — and my little girl nestles like a baby bird — *pretty as a picture* they used to say — and that's how we pass the morning — our cupcake back again — basking in the way it unspools — luxurious holiday rhythm — then gathering around the dining table — to write our notes of excuse — one for each of us — three truant schoolchildren — till that awful charwoman interrupts — telling us she's done for the day — only she won't leave — just hovering — *what is it?* I ask — *begging your pardon ma'am* she says — all proper like — *but you don't em need to bother yourselves* — *everything's been tended to* — waiting for us to ask about the details — hideous woman — *I'll just be going now* she says — hovering — *I'll just be on my way* — and when we don't answer — don't look up at her — she huffs and then the front door slams behind her — Papa raises his head — *well* he says in her wake — *she'll be given notice tonight* — we slip our notes into pretty envelopes — move wordless to the window, curtains wide, to watch the sky lightening over the church spires. Down on Charlotte Street people are filing into and out of the hospital. The rain has let up. It occurs to me it's going to be a beautiful day. Sometimes a person can tell. Geraniums. Little boys in sailor suits. We linger, clasping each other around the waist, admiring, taking pleasure in this string of breaths. A family.

papa

—Come along now, do, The Father proclaims, ease pervading him like the sunshiny haze gathering on the far side of the window.

He breaks his hold and announces everyone is to dress in his or her Sunday finest. Prepare a lunch fit for royalty. This will be a very special afternoon.

—Oh, dear, what on earth are we going to *do*? asks The Father's wife eagerly, hands nuzzled up beneath her chin, head tucked like a napping chicken's.

—Yes, Papa, *what*? asks Grete in her little girl's voice. Tell us! Tell us!

They are tramming into the countryside for a stroll and a picnic. For months they have been living in the sour paleness of anesthesia. Today that will be put behind them. It is time to wake up, time to rediscover the simple joys the world has to offer.

—But the *food!* cries The Father's wife, chicken head popping up. *The food!* There's none to waste, dear! We have difficulty enough obtaining the basics even as it is. How can we afford such a feast?

—Mutti's right, Grete chimes in, a note of concern stealing into her voice. Every morsel counts.

The Father's bonbon-brown eyes inspect them. This is his family. This is the kin he has been given. It will get no better. It will get no worse.

A slow smile inflates across his loose face.

—Ah, but this afternoon, he says tenderly, proudly—this afternoon is for thinking about other things. It is for feeling rich. Off you go now, both of you. I won't hear another word . . .

Outside, amid the shimmery residue of the fog, crowds pour onto the avenues lined with tree stumps. Although there remains a certain tentativeness to this communal gesture, a certain sense that everything everyone thinks could always be different than it is (and in the space between two ticks of a clock), what soon comes to matter more are the earthy, horsy fragrances spreading through the late morning, the growing vigor of the throngs, the sense of openness, opportunity, radiating good cheer.

Whatever happens will happen, The Father resolves to himself, making his way arm in arm with his wife and daughter, and the chances of it being something particularly unpleasant are quite remote at best.

Without a doubt, they have crossed the Rubicon.

He recalls with a sear of nostalgia mixed with vexation that this is the same sensation he experienced in the hub of his chest after lying awake in his cot all night in that stinking trench, listening to the *pop . . . pop . . . pop* coming across the no-man's land. The Father has seen things no man should have had to see, heard things no man should have had to hear, yet this is a fact: spring has reached the city, and spring is splendid. Sometimes that is all one can assert with any confidence.

Soon people will commence planting their own flowerbox gardens, raising ducks in spare rooms, moving into the outlying parks to cut and haul off wood in rattling wagons and rickety wheelbarrows against next winter. They will, in a word, get on with it, as people always do, despite the occasional ugliness, despite how weight has become an ever more important issue for some, despite the impression of hunchbacked calamity always wheezing just out of sight, up the next block, around the next corner, because this is how the species is put together. It is glued, wired, patched with odds and ends so that some will live to see the month after next.

We find our feet: this is what we are good at.

There is even talk of black-market fruits and vegetables, slipped across the border at night, starting to show up on carts in the alleys winding off squares near the castle. Things appear to be getting better and better. The Father closes his eyes and breathes the friendly scents around him deep into the bloom of his lungs.

In her free hand, his daughter carries the wicker basket heavy with sawdust-and-flour bread, shredded jackdaw meat, a tiny wedge of Brie, a third-full jar of stone-ground mustard, a small pungent diced onion, a bottle of inexpensive red wine, a tin of foie gras Mutti has been caching away since the Christmas before last, and a luscious plump fresh tomato the junior clerk presented to Papa last Friday as part of the week's payment (with, needless to say, no questions asked, no explanations given).

Mutti wears her very best dress, dark blue polka-dotted white, and carries a folded white-lace parasol that has seen somewhat better days. The intensifying sun hasn't persuaded her to open it yet.

Around them, pedestrians forge on into the heating morning, greeting each other, chattering, flirting, standing on street corners doing business, balancing children on their shoulders, stopping to ask after neighbors and friends they haven't seen since last autumn.

Striding with an august gait, The Father feels flanked by good fortune. He will not rush this. The world around him seems by degrees more airy. Yes, it goes without saying: he will jolly well fire that charwoman this evening. What is the point of maintaining help if it isn't worth a fig? Her caterwauling is quite appalling enough, thoroughly vulgar, but her crafty impertinence is altogether too much. It makes The Father feel . . . how does it make The Father feel? *Small.* That's how it makes The Father feel. And The Father refuses to feel small. He is not that kind of fellow.

Moreover, it occurs to him in an elated flash as they reach the tram stop, money the family holds back on that account could be applied toward other, more pressing matters. It is long past the hour to begin considering setting aside a little something for retirement. For the first time in years, the family is in a position to do so. Each of them possesses a reliable situation that appears likely to lead to more fruitful things. Too, immediate improvement in the family's circumstances could arise simply from moving into a smaller, cheaper flat. Why haven't they considered that before? Tomorrow morning, over toast and tea, The Father will start perusing the newspaper for affordable openings.

Extraordinary, thinks The Father, what a bit of thought and planning can accomplish.

Twenty minutes, and he is leaning back comfortably in his seat, the tram clippity-clapping around him. Narrow lanes choked with fellow citizens have shed away, replaced first by a cubist array of stark concrete tower blocks with boarded-up first- and second-story windows, soldiers milling around upended barrels out front, cooking over open fires ruddy bits

The Father can't quite distinguish, and then by the breached five-meter-tall defensive wall the military tried to throw up around the city in a failed eleventh-hour bid to keep the natural disasters at bay.

His daughter, his wife, and he are among the last passengers on board. At the far end of the car sit two elderly women holding hands, walking sticks resting against their lumpy bloodless knees. Their hair is the color of cotton candy. They appear to be praying or napping. Three seats behind them, four teenage boys are playing some sort of game. They toss a pair of dice on the floor, snort and guffaw at what fate has done to them, toss again. Across the aisle, a startlingly attractive woman in her early twenties stares expressionlessly out the window. She is overdressed for the day in a bulky black walking cape. Her hair, also black, is bobbed so that its lower pointy tips almost touch the corners of her mulberry mouth.

The tram passes through the dead zone the width of the city's river comprised of gray clayey earth where nothing grows, and enters with a blurry green rush the woods of the park.

Coming even with a sun-greased pond white-spotted with geese, The Father senses the tram beginning to lose speed. His daughter reaches forward to retrieve the family's picnic basket beneath her seat, and in those seconds The Father examines her unselfconsciously, delighting in the press of her firm young breasts against the fabric of her flowery summer dress, the way the line of her jaw expresses a determination it had not been capable of expressing only a few months earlier, the distance toward adulthood she has covered in less than a year.

All he used to think about her, and here she is, this person instead of any other. Delighting, he hardly notices the attractive woman in her early twenties reaching beneath her cape to extract something cumbersome and dangerous. Rather, he gives himself over to the sensation of the tram pulling into the stop restless with early-morning ramblers waiting to return to the city center, large glass birdcage of the café visible through softly greening branches beyond.

The Father gives himself over to the sensation of the doors folding open, of fresh, cool, grassy air wafting aboard.

Leaning forward to rise, he catches his wife's glance. She has been studying their daughter, too. They have been admiring her together. They exchange proud ghost grins, sharing a tribal secret by not sharing it.

grete

I can sense their cozy gaze upon me. It feels like a new layer of skin. Enjoying their enjoying, I swim in the vaporous blush behind my eyelids.

They say people travel either to find something or to lose something, but I wonder if maybe it isn't a little bit of both. The shock is how, returning from a foreign country, returning from crowded dreams or a piece of gorgeous music, you discover you are precisely the same person you were before setting off. Precisely the same person, and precisely a different person. Traveling always makes you at least two people at once. It is good for you, this doubleness. It allows you to see yourself as a stranger in your own mind.

Stretching, I see myself, briefly, a stranger sitting in the café where Herrmann and I first sat to get to know each other. Only it is half a year later, and the floor is littered with silverware and coffee-cup shards and a broken vase. Herrmann has left. I can feel it at the base of my spine: everything is backward. All the patrons are staring at me, waiting to see what I shall do next. What I shall do next is this: I shall reach down into my lap, pick up my napkin, dab my fingertips, fold it, place it neatly back on the table. What I shall do next is stand. The waiter will help me with my chair. I shall thank him civilly, retrieve my cane, and move toward the door with the smallest limp I can marshal.

On the street I shall put one foot in front of the other. That is how tomorrow arrives. All you have to do, I discover, is let it come.

I hold the picnic basket and cane before me, waiting for my parents to rise, thinking how tenses shift time from the future into the present every second. How next week I shall begin hunting for a flat. Something modest. Spare. I shall be the only one who possesses a key. Papa and Mutti may not appreciate my decision at the outset, but they will get used to it, learn to see how less space helps us make ends meet. It won't be very far from them. A five- or ten-minute stroll at most. It isn't distance that matters. It is the idea of distance.

The woman who has been sitting across from Papa hurries past me up the aisle. Maybe she is late for a date with her beau. I am taken by how pretty she is, her eyes the color of snow on an overcast day. Then I catch sight of the shiny brownish scab on her neck, a centimeter above her cape's collar. It is perhaps twice the size of Papa's, a fourth of Mutti's and mine.

Touching my own neck instinctively, it occurs to me that all across the city people are beginning to emerge from hibernation. It has been a long winter. My family has been through a lot.

We have returned to who we are. We have returned completely changed. We are where we have been. Everything is a version of something else.

We aren't alone.

Good, I think, limping down the aisle.

That's g—

margaret

Margaret leans back comfortably in her seat in the private room upstairs at the World's End reserved for meetings and small wedding receptions, cigarette smoke forming whitish nebulae in the air around her. Below, the bass and tinny snare from a folk-rock band and the put-on laughter of drinkers tipping back a few at the pub. The chinky tinking of glasses. Timothy leans forward to Margaret's right, clasped hands dangling between his spread khaki-trousered legs, deep into a conversation with the two elderly women across from him. Trying to follow along, Margaret decides she would describe the women's thinning curly poodle hair as the color of cotton candy. Five minutes ago they launched into an explanation of how Kafka believed human beings were God's nihilistic thoughts. They suggested readers might do well to consider Uwe the closest of the Samsas to the Almighty, a point that set Timothy off on an animated spiel about the thicket of irony texturing the novella in a manner that makes it practically impossible to pin down Kafka's position on any significant subject with anything like confidence, a remark that gave rise to the present wave of back-and-forth by the others—the well-groomed contract lawyer with a long whitepink razor-burned neck; the overweight socialist picking at a large wedge of boysenberry pie, often forgetting to swallow before offering up her own views; the bony, gray-skinned doctor, a recent widower for whom everything in Kafka's story is poignant; the outspoken Jamaican in her mid-thirties in the colorful rasta cap who divulged that she is an aspiring author, more than half finished with her first novel (a speculative fiction concerning Kafka she doesn't feel comfortable speaking about); the real estate agent with the buck-toothed porcelain veneers for whom everything in Kafka's story is comic; the business-woman in her early twenties wearing plum lipstick and a prim pleated skirt with a snug blouse who, given that hard glint in her wintry eyes, how she holds her cigarette like a surgical in-strument, Margaret guesses is into some serious B&D at the weekend; the small gravel-voiced teacher who enjoys nothing so much as lovingly explicating what she considers key passages in the book because, for her, all aerial views of fiction seem like giving answers on a calculus test without showing the actual work.

They have been at it for nearly an hour, and what Margaret has come to appreciate about them in that time is how they don't pressure you to perform, prove yourself. They welcome newcomers with a handful of tactful questions and cordial smiles, then settle down to talk about books. Two weeks ago it was Faulkner's *As I Lay Dying*. Two weeks from now it will be a novel called *Anxious Pleasures* by an author Margaret hasn't heard of.

Margaret finds these people nothing at all like the ones in those classes back at the poly. Just the opposite: they make her feel crackly and alert, and it has been a long while since she has felt crackly and alert. Buoyant, snug, she hardly notices the *pop . . . pop . . . pop*s splitting the night outside on Camden High Street. She gives herself over instead to the sensation of ideas lapping around her. How the overweight socialist follows everything she says with a lift of her right hand to her mouth, as if trying to catch her own laugh. How, although Margaret despises secondhand smoke, she deems the stuff here to smell oddly right, even cerebral in some stylish way. She gives herself over to the sensation of Timothy's considerable presence beside her, the band's bass in the pads of her feet. *Backfires*. It crosses her mind that must be what she is registering down in the street. *Backfires*.

She instinctively rubs her sore shoulder and stretches her young body, realizing, in the distance, as if spotting the spec of a supertanker far out on the glassy afternoon Atlantic, that she hasn't thought about her missing grandparents for hours.

And feels acutely guilty.

the neighbor

The author living alone in the flat directly below the Samsas coughs wetly in his sleep and rotates his head a little to the left. Lying on his back in his neatly made bed, hands fisted on belly, he dreams of an elderly couple lying side by side on their backs in a neatly made bed in a hotel room on a rainy island off the northwest coast. They are awake, holding hands in the dark, waiting, although they have forgotten what it is they are waiting for.

Their names are Neddie and Nellie. Two weeks ago they got into their small red Fiat to drive several kilometers to a party hosted by friends. At the second T in the road, they turned right instead of turning left. Their careful little lives fell away behind them. They had tidied their house, put out the rubbish, locked the windows. In the boot were two small dented leather suitcases. They meandered along narrow back roads through the night. To keep themselves awake, they sang songs popular when they first met. Dawn dusting the landscape, they pulled into an inexpensive hotel, rented a room, and slept. In each town through which they passed, they stopped at the local chemist to purchase over-the-counter drugs they read about in a special book they ordered from America. The only way they remembered to do so was by taping to the dashboard the instructions they had written down.

After traveling like that for nearly a week, Neddie and Nellie ran out of land. They took a ferry across to an island, drove until they reached the far side, took another ferry, and so on. Before long, they ran out of ferries. They took a room at this hotel, a whitewashed rectangular box with a dark slate roof set atop a barren promontory overlooking a sea the color of slick stones and opals.

Three heartflutters ago, they awoke from dreaming the same dream. In it, an elderly couple noticed one day they had begun losing weight. They had been quite fit. They ate well. They got plenty of rest. Yet no matter what they did, they couldn't help it. They shed the smallest amounts at first. So small, they took unspoken pride in their unintentional accomplishment. But the losses mounted. Each morning they stepped onto the scale to discover there was just a little less of them than there had been the morning before.

Then it struck them: they were not losing fat. They were losing memories. Every day a handful more burned away like so many unwanted calories. In the beginning, it was nothing to get alarmed about: the misplaced car keys, the sack of groceries accidentally left behind on the supermarket counter. They told each other not to worry. It happened to everyone. Slowly, though, matters became more serious. The unrenewed subscriptions piled up, the unpaid bills. The couple couldn't recall the names of their friends, then of their grandchildren. They hadn't thought of their favorite, Margie, for weeks.

Yesterday they noticed when attempting to walk that their feet only touched the carpet sporadically. This morning the best they could do was float a little above it, as if there were an invisible floor hovering three centimeters atop the real one. Sometime early this afternoon, in the middle of a conversation about where the wife might have left her reading glasses, they were unnerved when their heads bumped against the ceiling.

They had become that light. It was tricky for them to reach the dining room table to eat, but they told themselves that that was all right because they didn't have much of an appetite left anymore anyway.

They kissed with a familiar kiss only those married for many decades can fully appreciate, and, crawling upside down across the ceiling, inched their way to the window, which the husband, after a bit of logistical nuisance, pried open. Holding hands, they eased through. Up they ascended into the cool night sky blurry with stars. They became smaller and smaller as they rose, at first the size of dolls, then fists, then thumbs, then teeth, and then they vanished altogether—and then Neddie and Nellie opened their eyes in this hotel room in this whitewashed rectangular box.

They lie quietly side by side in a neatly made bed, trying to figure out if this is the dream or the other thing.

—Where are we? Nellie asks in the darkness.

—I don't know, Neddie replies.

He sits up cautiously and pats the air around him until he locates a light switch at the base of a lamp on the side table. To the best of his recollection, he has never seen this lamp or this room before. Taped to the base by the switch he finds a list of instructions written in what he recognizes as his own handwriting. He plucks it off and reads it aloud with interest. Nellie concentrates, asking him to repeat certain phrases she finds difficult to take in.

They do what the instructions tell them: fill glasses of water at the sink in the corner and swallow the pills they bought on their journey. They become drowsy. When their muscles begin loosening, their breaths become shallower, they turn off the lamp and lie down in the dark once more and, once more, take each other's hands. Soon they can no longer tell if they have started to sleep or are still awake. Neddie looks around, confused. He is positive he sees the luminous outline of a tall skinny man sitting naked in the chair by the telly at the foot of the bed. The man is watching them. Nellie has the distinct impression Neddie and she are bobbing on a raft in the middle of a very calm ocean on a very clear night. She can hear the waves lapping around them. When she starts feeling uneasy, she rolls onto her side and curls into Neddie's thin arms. She enjoys the sour-milk fragrance of his mouth.

The tall skinny man at the foot of the bed stands, approaches them, leans over Nellie and, running his fingers through her hair, whispers *heart of my heart, heart of my heart,* until Nellie no longer feels frightened. Her body seems to her less and less significant, like a large hand has begun to erase it.

—What time is it? she asks, although a second later she can't remember having just asked.

The sound of the windy drizzle outside suffuses the room and then, from a very long way off, from a centimeter to her left, from deep inside her head, a voice resonant with kindness and reassurance replies:

—Let me see, angel. It's . . . it's a quarter to seven. It's already a

acknowledgments

Those familiar with Kafka's work will notice my periodic skirting of his language and stories here. Throughout, I use my own translations. The ideas in the first "margaret reading" chapter are from Guy Debord's *The Society of the Spectacle;* their application to Kafka is my own. The first section of the third "margaret reading" chapter is a slight revision of the first paragraph of Albert Camus's essay, "Hope and the Absurd in the Work of Franz Kafka"; the third and fourth sections are almost-quotes from Guy Davenport's essay, "The Hunter Gracchus"; parts of the last section are indebted to Curtis White's thesis in *The Middle Mind.* The quote by Carole Maso in the fifth "margaret reading" chapter is from her essay, "World Book." Ernst Pawel's *The Nightmare of Reason: A Life of Franz Kafka* provides biographical details that I have appropriated and skewed in various ways throughout. An excerpt from this novel originally appeared in *Sleepingfish.*

author bio

Lance Olsen studied at the University of Wisconsin, the Iowa Writers Workshop, and the University of Virginia. He is the author of eight novels, four short story collections, and several books of criticism. His stories, essays, poems, and reviews have appeared in hundreds of journals, magazines, and anthologies. Olsen is an NEA fellowship and Pushcart Prize recipient, and his novel *Tonguing the Zeitgeist* was a finalist for the Philip K. Dick Award. He serves as chair of the board of directors at Fiction Collective Two; founded in 1974, FC2 is one of America's best known ongoing literary experiments and progressive art communities. Olsen lives with his wife, assemblage-artist Andi Olsen, in the mountains of central Idaho. More information is available at www.lanceolsen.com.

Printed in the United States
by Baker & Taylor Publisher Services